Revelation
at the Snows

A. Jay

ISBN 978-1-64471-594-9 (Paperback)
ISBN 978-1-64471-595-6 (Digital)

Covenant Books, Inc.
11661 Hwy 707
Murrells Inlet, SC 29576
www.covenantbooks.com

A deceiving smile lures the innocent to their destruction.
Good overcomes evil then we win.

Dedication

Virginia "Ginny" Haines
May 22, 1927–July 22, 2018

I would like to dedicate this novel to Ginny Haines, her family originally was from Agrigento, Italy, and her birth name was Vecenza Catolica. Vecenza Catolica's character was created with her in mind who was a famous baker in her day, especially for her apple pies. Her wish was to have a bit character in this novel. This special lady was the mother of a very close friend, Nancy Haines Barron. Ginny will not be forgotten.

Acknowledgments

I would like to acknowledge Marvin Chard for permission to use historical facts about his lumber mill as well as facts about his father. Bruce J. Dodson at the Dodson Funeral home in St. Ignace gave the history of the funeral and autopsy location at the era in the novel. Also June Maurer, a retired teacher and friend, for her help with editing and suggestions. Michele Fick Fiering, my daughter, was helpful with suggestions and critiques. And finally, I wish to give acknowledgment to Russell Sherlund for giving me historical information on the Les Cheneaux area.

Prologue

The Mackinaw Bridge was reaching finalization that would connect Lower Michigan to the Upper Peninsula of Michigan. Many would come to inhabit the quiet world in the north, but even before the opening, a few stragglers came via Wisconsin to settle in the eastern end of the UP.

George Kaughman, the local sheriff's life was quiet with very few incidents interfering with his routine life. He and his wife, Maria, still lived in the Cedarville area and were blessed with a six-year-old daughter, Susan.

They were planning to attend the grand opening of the Mackinaw Bridge when the call came in...

Chapter One
Anna Belle's Flight

Anna Belle woke with a start. She was in a strange bed, with no clothing on. She knew she had to escape quickly. She listened for her abductor. He was nowhere near. She grabbed a shirt that hung over the bedpost. She quickly threw it on and ran out the kitchen door toward the road. The gravel hurt her foot, as she only had one shoe on. She reached the edge of the sandy road and ran in the direction that she thought her home was. When she reached the end of the road, there were only two ways to go, either north or south. She looked straight ahead at a field of hay and tall grass that had not been mowed or pastured off for a long time. She stumbled over a rut as she tried to cross the road. The ditch was deep on the other side, so she jumped across. Her feet landed on dry grass, hurting her bare foot, yet she continued.

Just as she reached the woods, she could hear the motor of his truck echo across the still night air. She ducked when she saw the headlights flash in her direction. In panic, she lunged into the woods and kept on running. Across the field and woods, she could hear the truck racing up the road and back as her abductor searched for her. Her heart pounded in fear when she heard the truck motor become silent.

She knew he was running through the field after her. She had reached the next road, crossed it, and continued racing as fast as she could through it. She heard the snapping of branches as his long legs quickly thrashed his way toward her.

The moon suddenly broke through the clouds. She knew it would be just a matter of time that he would find her. Looking around she saw the moonlight resting on a huge fallen hollowed out tree. It was moss covered and large enough for her to crawl up into it. She inched herself up into the tree as far as she possibly could. She pulled the moss back over her as she attempted to conceal her location. She began to shiver in fear and cold. He was very near. She was certain he could hear her heart pound in her chest. She held her breath when he stopped near the tree. Then she felt nothing as darkness enveloped her.

* * * * *

It was late afternoon on a warm day in September in the fall of 1953. The uneventful day kept George the local deputy sheriff cleaning and filing in his office. He enjoyed watching across at his wife working on the newspaper, the *Weekly Wave*. He shared the building with her, giving George one third of the building, which was her father's office before he died. The sheriff substation contained a temporary holding cell, his desk, a couple of chairs, and filing cabinets. A picture of Abe Lincoln hung behind him on the wall, the opposite wall held an old Ingram pendulum clock, and there was a woodburning stove to keep the office warm in the winter.

George almost jumped as the wall phone shattered the silence.

"Hello, George, this is Ralph. I am calling because of daughter Anna Belle. She didn't come home from school this afternoon. My wife, Martha, is near hysterical. We both knew about the other girls and now Anna Belle didn't return from school. We're really upset, can you help us?"

"I'll be right over. We need to follow her bus route while it is still light out to look for footprints alongside the road. I'll get there as quick as possible, Ralph."

George picked up Ralph, and Martha Carter fifteen minutes later. They drove the bus route backward from their farm along the roads the bus had taken. Driving slowly, they watched for footprints and signs of struggle, to no avail. They stopped at the bus driver's home to see if he could tell them something.

Old Joe stepped out on the porch and lifted his cap to scratch his head. "What brings you folks here?"

George told him what they were doing and wondered if he could give them a clue as to if Anna Belle rode the bus or got off along the route at her friend's home.

Joe looked a little guilty when he responded. "She wanted to get off and walk through the woods home. The last I saw through the rearview windows she was walking along the sandy road."

"She didn't make it home!" Martha screamed at him.

"Show us where you dropped her off, Joe," George calmly asked him.

Joe jumped into his pickup and said, "Follow me."

From Joe's home and over the roads toward the Carter farm took nearly three quarters of an hour. Approximately one mile from their farm across the woods, tracks were on the road of Anna Belle's shoe prints, but they abruptly stopped. There were tire tracks and her footprints appeared to stop when she got into the vehicle.

The tire tracks had been overlapped from other automobiles leaving no trace of what direction Anna Belle had gone in.

George took Martha and Ralph back to the farm. "I won't be able to see well enough tonight, so I'm going to call it quits until daylight tomorrow morning. I promise I'll be here at the crack of dawn. Please try to get some rest. Pray and wait for his answer. I will do the same for your daughter and you two. I know what you are going through. I don't have the proper equipment to go right now, unless you have any ideas."

"Our dog can. He can find anything. All we have to do is have him smell her clothes and we can find her."

"I'll stay home and finish the chores," Martha said. "I won't be any good out there anyway."

George quickly called his wife, Maria, and told her not to wait up. He told her briefly what he was doing, and they were ready to go. Ralph, George, and the dog drove over to the spot where they thought she disappeared. The dog sniffed and followed her footprints until he stopped and began to go in circles. The dog looked lost, the trail stopped, he couldn't find her.

They drove back to the farm. It wasn't long that the dog began running toward the woods across the hayfield. The two men followed the dog. Even though they were tired the adrenaline flowed with the urgency and will to find Anna Belle.

As soon as they crossed a large acreage they entered the woods. The moon appeared then went under clouds. It was dark and hard to see very far ahead. They thought they heard something like branches snapping. The dog barked. They could hear more noise like running away. "It probably was a deer," Ralph said.

The dog didn't follow the deer. Instead, he headed in the opposite direction. He began to bark again. This time the dog was barking frantically. He kept running around a tree that had fallen and moss had grown over it. He began to dig at the moss while barking. Then he looked at George and Ralph and barked while he poked his head into the hollow tree. George saw white when the moon came out just enough to tell there was something inside the tree. He and Ralph both fell on their knees and helped each other get Anna Belle out of the tree. She was unconscious. George cradled her in his arms and carried her back to the farmhouse.

* * * * *

George drove Anna Belle to the hospital in St. Ignace. Ralph and Martha followed behind with their truck.

George was deep in thought. Anna Belle was the third victim. (Except she was alive, barely. The first two died.) Was it the same person who did this he asked himself? I need to catch this monster before anything more happens here.

* * * * *

Six years had passed since the shocking death of his best friend, Two Shoes. George's loss had been comforted by the love of his friend Maria. He smiled when he remembered the day they were married. She made a beautiful bride that day when she became his wife. Little Susie was born the following February. He felt complete for the first time in a very long while.

He remembered how this nightmare began on an August day, approximately a year and a half earlier. George heard his phone ring in the sheriff office.

Chapter Two
Unexpected Call

"George, this is Bill Catolica, over here on Webb Road. I was on my way home from mowing hay down the Miller Farm Road and around the corner. I was driving the Minneapolis Moline tractor when I saw it. I was by the old haunted Miller farm when I noticed something in the ditch on the opposite side of the farm that looked like a small body. I jumped from the tractor and looked closer to find blood everywhere and what appeared to be a dead girl."

"What? Where are you calling from?"

"I frantically ran down the road to the first farm to let you know right away. I'm at Martin Fletcher's farm."

"Stay right there, I'll pick you up on the way."

"Good, because I was so shocked I ran on foot all the way here and left the tractor running."

George quickly dialed up Drake, the undertaker and pathologist in St. Ignace, to tell him what had happened and asked him to meet him on the Miller Road.

George grabbed tape, his camera, and his print case. He had paced the floor all the while he talked to Bill. Now he called across to his wife, "Honey, I have to go. Don't hold supper for me. It's going to take quite a while for me this time."

He threw a kiss to her and his three-year-old daughter Susie. "What... I know, you can't tell me until it is solved. We'll be waiting for your return."

George headed west of Cedarville to the crossroad at Hessel Village where he turned north on Three Mile Road to Dixie Highway, turning left at the Runway Bar. He saw five cars and two pickups were parked outside. He reached Webb Road and headed north following the road as it curved, and soon he was picking Bill up at the Fletcher farm. George drove the mile to the spot where Bill found the body.

Martin Fletcher's place on Webb Road was a mile down the road from the crime site. The old farm across the way was deserted and had been for quite some time. Windows were broken in the old farmhouse, while doors hung on by one hinge swinging in the wind. The windmill was bent with parts missing as well. The huge old barn was sagging in midroof. Tall grass had yellowed and made the place appear deserted. Only the curved gravel driveway seemed the same.

* * * * *

Meanwhile, the perpetrator sat on his small porch thinking that evening. *I wish Ma hadn't died. I miss her cooking. Dad died first, then her. What am I thinking? It's good to be free of always falling over them? Ma continually whined about supper being cold because I didn't come home on time. What's on time? And him, the old man, always sitting there next to the radio blaring loudly because his hearing wasn't as good as it used to be. Television was out of the question, we couldn't afford one. The price was out of our range, and so was the reception here anyway.*

So I can come home, and while I still sleep in the basement, I can have the whole house to myself.

That day, after having his way with the girl—the struggle, the screams, the rock—he looked down at his trousers and thought, *I'll have to wash the blood off my clothing, a little here on my cuff and... darn, spots all over my new coveralls and shoes too. It's all her fault. All of it! She lured me into desire that only a man can know. If she wouldn't have screamed so loud, I wouldn't have had to quiet her. Shut her trap. Smashing her head with that rock a few times made her quiet. She asked for it.*

* * * * *

George drove west on Webb Road and followed it along the deep sandy ruts as they curved and turned on the Miller Road, driving until he could see the hip roof of the old Miller barn. His eyes looked away from the barn to the spot a little farther up the road where he saw the hump of a body lying in the ditch.

He turned the ignition off and sat a moment, taking the entire view in. He didn't want to miss any detail of the scene. He loaded his camera, stepped out of the truck, and walked closer to take several pictures of the murder scene.

Yes, there was little doubt that the tiny girl was dead, as rigor mortis had set in by this time, in that strange curled-up position. He touched a cold, stiff body. As he rolled her body over, her knees protruded in the air. He discovered from all appearances she had fallen and hit her head on a rock, which lay under her head. The blood had splashed over her head and upper torso. There also was dried blood on her thighs and legs. She appeared to be abused and assaulted. *Too much blood for just falling, definitely foul play*, George thought.

George took more pictures and looked for any identification to prove who this young girl was. He would have to get positive identification for the records.

At that time Drake drove up the road from St. Ignace with his hearse. Drake had taken the Dixie Highway to Simmons Road, followed the sandy curves on Webb Road toward the old farmhouse, where he saw George.

Drake's curved handled pipe stuck between his teeth as he bit down hard on it. The only time he took it out was to talk, which he did at present. "What do we have here, George? Oh, crap, not a child?"

"Afraid so, Drake, she can't be over thirteen years old."

"Whoever did this is evil and very sick." He stood for the longest time, looking at her with a sad expression on his face. "Well, George, help me load her up." He reached for a blanket to wrap her, gently rolled her over on the stretcher, and the two placed her in the back of the wagon. "When you get her identification, call me, and let me know. Till then she will be a question mark." He shook his head. "Bad business, George, what's this, your second in thirteen years as a deputy sheriff?"

"Yes, but this is worse than the last, even if it was my friend then. A defenseless child is more than anyone can understand."

Drake held his hat in his hands, out of respect to this child. It seemed the natural thing to do. George looked up to see a tear sit on the edge of Drake's eye. He blinked it away and turned toward his cab.

"Drake, I know how you feel, I have a three-year-old girl. If this ever happened to her, I'd want to tear him limb to limb."

"I'll say, and I hope and pray that never happens, George." With that said, he stepped into the driver's seat and drove away.

Looking once again at the matted grass and the bloody rock, George shook the fingerprint dust over the smooth sandstone rock and lifted a couple of clear prints. That was a good step in the right direction. Now the investigation had begun. He placed the rock in an evidence bag and laid it on the floor in the back.

The sun was setting when George drove into Bill Catolica's yard. George had followed Bill home since it was getting late and there were no lights on the tractor. The two men stopped and sat on the front porch. George wanted to talk more to him about what he discovered and ask him if there was anything else he could remember that may be pertinent to the event of the girl's death. George could smell the odor of Bill's wife baking. Vincenza Catolica was famous for her pies and pastries. She supplied all the local restaurants. The tourists looked forward to their vacation just to have a pastry with coffee or a piece of pie after the evening meal. George heard Vincenza hum to herself as she worked in the kitchen.

"Bill, I'm hoping you can tell me some bit of information that will give me a lead."

"No, I only found her. You see, George, and the girl was there long before I went over to that field to cut hay. The weather was perfect for haying. It said on the radio that morning there would be clear skies until August 15, so I decided that now was the time to get it done. And just in time for the fair, we always go, you know, eh?"

"What makes you think she was there long before you found her, Bill?"

"The blood, it was dry. She must have been there from the night before."

"Did you notice anything else that was strange about this incident?"

"Oh, George, I did forget that I found her schoolbag lying next to the driveway when I went into the field this morning. I didn't think much about it at the time, but now I think it may have been hers."

"Why didn't you think of it? We need to know who she is, something to verify who she is. So I better leave to drive back to the field to look for it."

"The schoolbag is right here, but you aren't going to know who she is, there isn't a thing in it."

George was doing everything to control his feelings at this point. Bill was exasperating him. "You looked in the bag?"

"Err, well, yes, I thought I'd find something…but there wasn't anything in it."

"Do you realize you could be charged with tampering with evidence? You could have erased finger prints, or yours will be the only ones on the bag. I may have to arrest you until I find that you are innocent of this horrific crime."

"No, hell no, I didn't do it. I only messed with the bag."

"Bill, I hope you realize what you did by tampering with evidence."

Bill looked down at the porch floor and said, "I guess I was curious, and it caused me to do exactly what I shouldn't have. I'm sorry, but I hope you don't think I did this. I never could harm a child. Life means too much to me."

"It's okay, Bill, just think first before you do something like this again."

Vincenza stepped out on the porch. "Excuse me, Sheriff George, you have a phone call from the County Sheriff office."

"George, we got a call from Gordon and Jane Adams saying that their girl didn't come home yesterday or today. So, we believe our Jane Doe is Jenny Adams, the nine-year-old who Drake brought in this evening. She is big for her age and was easily mistaken for a teenager on the loose. It's bad that she is dead. This girl lived on the eastern end of the county, nowhere near the murder location."

"Thanks for the information. It will give me something to begin with." He hung up and looked at the Catolicas and said, "We believe this girl was one that her parents reported missing. I will go over to see them right now. Thank you, Bill, for your help." He nodded at Vincenza and said, "Good evening." George touched his hat and left.

George knew he needed to relax and slowly watch for clues as each day passed. It was his daughter, Susie, he thought of. She would be four soon. If anything like this ever happened to her, it would be difficult to handle. He reflected as he traveled back to Cedarville. *We have a sick man on the loose. I need to find him. The first thing I will do is ask around to see if anyone has seen anyone who is unusually different and questionable. Jeffery would be the one, he never missed much.*

For the second time in George's career, he had the chore of telling the parents their child was dead. The couple lived north through the cedar swamps to the hardwood area on a curve, with a lovely home nestled back in a grove of young maples. George drove in the horseshoe drive, strode the few feet to the steps to the front porch, and knocked on the door. He was greeted by Mr. Adams.

"You found her, you found Jenny." Gordon ran to meet George. Jane came running behind Gordon both anxious to hear the news.

George looked directly into his eyes and told Mr. Adams gently, "First of all, I'm not sure the girl that was found is your daughter, Jenny. You will have to go in to St. Ignace to the coroner Drake and make sure it is or isn't her. I will go with you if you wish."

"Yes, we would like you to go with us." They both agreed.

The drive to St. Ignace took just over thirty minutes to get there. George, Gordon, and Jane entered Drake's office.

"Drake, this is Gordon and Jane Adams. They're here to identify the Jane Doe you brought in earlier today. Their daughter has been missing since after school yesterday."

Drake shook each parent's hand and said she was in the next room. "Follow me and I will show you her face to help you decide if it is your daughter."

Jane held Gordon's hand tightly in fear that it was her daughter. She shook uncontrollable with anticipation. Gordon held her hand while he put his arm around her waist. Drake pulled out the body, which was on a cot covered with a white sheet. Drake looked up at the couple as he pulled back the sheet from her face.

A gasp was heard from Jane. "Oh, my baby girl, my god in heaven, why?" Jane slumped to the floor in a faint. Gordon caught her, cushioning her fall. Pain in his eyes showed his grief, even though he was trying to be brave for his wife. He hid his tears and held her while Drake gave her smelling salts to revive her.

It took a few minutes for Jane to face the reality of the fact that her daughter was victimized. "Tell us everything, we need to know where and what happened. We want that killer, the evil one who did this to our daughter. Tell us, George." Jane began to sob again.

Gordon comforted her, "There, there darling, be calm, George is doing everything he can."

They both looked at George waiting for a response.

"Your daughter was found by a farmer, Bill Catolica. Do you know him?"

Gordon replied, "We know who he is." Jane nodded.

George began the tale of discovery. "Bill was taking the shortcut home from mowing hay around four yesterday. He found a girl lying in the ditch. He looked closer to see that she wasn't sleeping. He reported what he found after he ran on foot to the nearest neighbor to call me."

A tear rested on Jane's cheekbone, as she sat silently holding back her pain. Gordon looked straight out the window. "Tell us everything, George, we need to know."

"At first, it appeared that she fell and hit her head on a stone. There was blood in her hair and around that area as well as on the ground under her head. Looking closer, I discovered her clothing had been ripped off her, with blood on the dress and undergarment, including her thighs and legs as well."

Jane let out a gasp, Gordon held her close, and sobs began again.

George waited until they were ready to hear more. He hated to be too graphic, so if they asked, then he would tell more. It was a sordid tale. A sociopath was on the loose in the small remote area in the Eastern Upper Peninsula of Michigan. George held back fury that was suppressed to keep his head clear in order to find leads and clues. This man, this animal, needed to be caught and brought to justice.

"Tell us everything, we deserve to know." Jane and Gordon sat with crestfallen expression. Jane's eyes were red and swollen. Jane sounded like a broken record that kept repeating. She was in shock.

"I have told you all I know for now. I'm sorry for your loss. As soon as the examination is complete here in St. Ignace, I will let you know. At that time, I will be able to tell when you can make arrangements for her funeral and burial." George stood and replaced his hat on his curly blond head of hair. "I'm truly sorry for your loss. I will not rest until this has closure. It's a dastardly deed that has been done to Jenny, and I pray it is the last. This guy is on the loose, and he needs to be caught."

Jane and Gordon led the way to the car while George followed. The men sat in front while Jane sat in the back seat staring into space.

Chapter Three
August Funeral

Back in town, George found his very pregnant wife and daughter, who slept lying on the couch. He told her of little Jennifer and enough information to print an obituary and a small news article about the discovery and death of this unfortunate child.

A few days later, cars lined both sides of Bay Street, near and around the Union Church. Family, friends, and curiosity seekers attended the funeral of Jennifer Rose Adams, a nine-year-old girl, who would be laid to rest in the local cemetery on four-mile block.

It was a hot day in August in an area that hardly ever saw the temperature climb to ninety degrees. Women wore various shades of black and wide-brimmed hats, gloves, and heels. The men wore various clothing, but most of them dressed in their Sunday-go-meeting suits. The church building bulged at the seams with the crowd. Many had to sit on seats that lined the walk outdoors. The double front doors swung wide and propped open so they could hear the sermon.

Flowers decked the entire front of the church, leaving a small spot for the pastor to stand. Fat ladies were fanning themselves. Men were mopping their brow with white handkerchiefs. Family cried throughout the entire service; many just looked and listened. Some wore fear on their faces, wondering if the killer was there among them. Others merely desired to be a part of the gathering and to get a free dinner.

Children of all ages attended, especially teenagers. The youth wore various colors of pastel, and the boys wore jeans. The shock of Jenny's loss left fear in their heart. Some held hatred for the one responsible for what was done to her. *It won't happen to me, I'll be ready for him. We'll get that guy,* the boys thought.

George watched for any clue that indicated a possible suspect. He decided to talk to the principal as soon as possible. He made a note of it in his book pad.

As the day waned away, a service was completed, flowers loaded in the hearse and taken to the grave, and finally the group of mourners ended back at the church for a very fine dinner. Many sat and visited, talking about how she would miss out on an entire life, many speculated who it may have been that did the crime. George listened to as many conversations as he could, searching for logic in their suspicions. The sun had come around, and the afternoon was almost gone. One at a time, the crowd began to dwindle, some people walked. Others drove a new green hardtop Chevrolet, a Pontiac with stripes along the hood, or a yellow-and-white Ford. There was even a good old reliable jalopy.

George recalled how he went to visit the principal the very next day after the funeral. Joseph Johnson shook George's hand and said, "Have a seat. I can guess why you are here, so come right out with it."

"I came to talk with you about Jenny. Who did she chum with? Please include males and females alike. Also from your observation, did she have any enemies, or a male friend she may have rejected? I know she was only nine, but she appeared to be older because of her maturity."

"From my experience, she had few friends and seemed happy for the ones she did have." Johnson leaned forward and wrote a few names down on a paper tablet. He erased one and said, "This may be helpful." Joe Johnson handed the list to George as he rose to follow the deputy to the door.

George watched the listed youngsters whenever he could, which included sports events, stage plays, and band concerts. He felt he was watching for absolutely nothing. *Boys always snicker when they are talking about girls. It's not a crime. Girls were another story because of jealousy they may have a reason*, George thought. *But most of all, unless the chick was sick, it was only surface jealousy and not something to worry about. It didn't jive. This girl was molested and murdered. A girl would have to be older and really sick to have done this to Jenny.*

Three months had passed. Nothing led George to clues that would help him solve who murdered the child. Other daily duties kept George from searching any farther with the young Adams girl's death. He did however have a list made of the speculations made at the funeral that day. His conversation with Jeffery helped him make a list of those he wasn't aware of, such as recluses, single men who didn't live a normal life or had a secret life not shared with others. He would look it over and try to match it to the people he knew in the farthest east area of Drummond Island to as far west as Moran. Not many to pick from that would fit the description of a person who would do this kind of act.

He had contact with Lightfoot, his Native American friend who spent time with him. Lightfoot was a busy man as well, keeping peace among the Anishinabek he was in charge of. It was an honor to have a few minutes with him as busy as he was. He promised to keep an eye out for anything that appeared unusual or strange.

Chapter Four
Following Hunches and Suspicions

Other daily duties kept George from searching any farther with the young Adams girl's death. He did however have a list of his speculations at the funeral. The character George suspected would appear quiet, many times polite to his peers, he would show respect, but to discern what is normal behavior or what is not was difficult for anyone. George decided to talk to each suspect in a friendly manner and talk about each one's personal life.

His list included Chester "Chet" Wilson, who spends his days taking care of a herd of Mackinac Island horses in the winter at his forty-acre plot of land and helps with the horses on the island in the summer. He lives in a small log-style cabin off to the east near a camp for local school students. He was a prime interest because of the connection. George had been watching him, what he did and where he went for a while. Even though he kept to himself, he was seen periodically at the Cedarville Bar. He never spoke to anyone much and left after a couple of drinks. George made it a point to go out to see him just a few days after the murder took place.

After the third attempt to find him home, George finally found him in the backyard splitting wood.

"Hello, George, what brings you out this way?" Chet shouted across the yard to the approaching sheriff.

"Hello, Chet, I stopped over twice before, you're a hard man to find home."

"I keep busy, George, moss doesn't grow under my feet."

"I came out to talk to you about the little Adams girl. Did you know her?"

"I did see her when she was at the camp last summer, but I didn't know her. Really, you know, when I saw her picture in the paper, I recognized her as one of the kids out there camping. Why?"

"I'll be direct." Chet's eyes glazed in fear. George caught it even though Chet quickly covered it. "Do you remember what you were doing a couple weeks ago when Jenny was murdered?"

"When was she murdered?"

"You did read the papers, didn't you? It was over a week and a half ago, say ten days ago, or so. She was found by Bill Catolica."

Ten days ago, he thought, then he answered George's question. "I was still on the island, I would be there now, but I had to come home for a personal reason."

"Do you mind telling me what that personal reason was?"

"Yes, sir, I do, I really don't want to share it with you, but if you insist, I needed to see the doctor."

"Can I ask you what the reason was?"

"I have a very serious infection, and he has given me some sulfur to help clear it up. I'm not willing to try that penicillin because too many people are allergic to it. You know, they only discovered it in 1929, and that's not too long ago."

George looked him over and wanted to ask him where the infection was. He noticed he had a scrape on his face, like he possibly could have been in a fight. "Is it because of the scrape on your face, how did that happen?"

"Barbed wire fence. No, it's somewhere else."

"Okay, I won't ask you where that somewhere else is unless I need to know. I'll be checking back in a few days to see how you're doing. When are you returning to the island?"

"Tomorrow morning."

George nodded and turned to leave. Chet called to him, "I didn't have anything to do with that girl."

The second suspect on George's list was a man named Maxwell Stewart. He lived on Little La Salle Island and was somewhat of a recluse. George and almost everyone else knew very little about him. The information from Jeffery was that he had retired early in his life, was somewhere between the age of fifty to sixty years old, and remained on the little island unless he needed to come on the mainland to get supplies or attend church, which he did regularly. He was a man with little to say and seemed to avoid talking to those who approached him at the afterglow when church was over. He obviously seen the little old ladies approaching him, so he turned on his heel and rushed out the door. George had talked to the minister to gather some of this information. Now it was time to take the trek out to Little LaSalle Island to have a talk with him.

As top priority on his list, it was George's intention to go out there sometime in the coming week. He never expected the unusual. It was time for George and Maria's next child to be born.

He looked back through the nine months she carried his daughter. Maria was pregnant again for their second child. She was beautiful even when she was in that condition. Her cheeks were rosy, and her eyes glowed in a special way that enhanced her already handsome features. It seemed as though this condition was exactly what it took to bring out the very best in her.

Fortunately her pregnancy didn't keep her from doing her job of putting out the newspaper. It came out each week regularly. There always were newsy items to read along with reviews and special editorials. Once in a while she would print a short story supplied by a local writer. It was called the feature story of the week.

George went fishing during the summer more than the winter. And many a day he went with his friend Rob Lightfoot. The lazy days of summer turned into fall with very few incidents between to keep George busy, yet his thoughts kept coming back to the murder. He soon found it took a lot of patience to solve this kind of murder.

For one thing, he spent most of his time watching every person who lived in the area. He would cruise the area just observing who was visiting who, how long, and what they were there for. The best thing was his friend Jeffery Beacom, who seemed to see as much and carried his stories in to George on a weekly pattern.

Jeffery had lots to say, but nothing he said seemed to a correlate with the dead girl. Not anything near it. It seemed to George like a dead end. There wasn't any similarity to the search for his friend's murder a few years earlier.

Watching was his only way to find the culprit. He had asked many of the schoolmates if they remembered anything that she may have told them. They had exactly nothing to tell. He also asked the family and the neighbors on either side of them if they knew or saw anything out of the ordinary. He still found nothing. The case wasn't closed, but it definitely went cold.

* * * * *

The ride into St. Ignace hospital with his wife beside him was silent. "Honey are you okay?" he asked her, realizing he was deep in thought.

"I'll do all right, I'm glad you were in your office when the first warning pain occurred. I don't know what I would have done if you were out talking to suspects." She smiled at him.

"I'm glad too, I wouldn't miss this for the world, honey." He looked her way, relieved. "I love you so much, Maria, you have made me so happy. You are a good wife and mother. We're going to have to get a helper in the news office after this one is born. You'll need the help."

"We'll talk about that after the baby is born, George. It was good of your mom to get Susie until you return."

"Until we return," George retorted. "I'm not leaving you there even for one moment, unless you stay for a month."

"George, quit teasing." She laughed through her pain. "Oh... George, they're getting stronger."

"We're almost there, honey. Hold your britches."

He gently cradled Maria into his arms and carried her into the yellow old mansion hospital, where the nurses took over. "You just stay out here in this waiting room, George. We'll call you when it's over." The short fat nurse clucked at him. The doctor came from the other room with white clothing and a towel drying his hands. He nodded at George and entered the delivery room.

Chapter Five
A New Quest

The evil one had watched the woman next door for a month. Actually "next door" wasn't close, across the sandy road on an angle from his home. He could see her nevertheless. He was getting sick about not having made an acquaintance with her. One day, he noticed she struggled with a stump. She was trying to remove it by digging then using a wedge and sledge to split it a few pieces away at a time.

"Can I help you with that?" he asked her.

She jumped away from him startled, not suspicious that anyone was near. "Oh, you startled me."

"Don't be afraid, I just wish to help you," he said. "You probably haven't seen me before because I work long hours. I live across the road." He pointed at the home that was on an angle from her house.

She peered in that direction, took a deep breath, and said, "Yes, I do need help."

After a few blows to the sledge, the stump came out roots and all. "There, I think this will do."

"Thank you, can you come in for a cup of tea and some cookies?"

The sucker, he thought. "Sure, I'll need to wash my hands first though."

She answered by saying, "You can wash them here. The bathroom is off the kitchen to the right."

She washed in the kitchen sink, boiled the water, and poured it over the tea bags in the teapot to steep. He came out of the bathroom smiling at her. She placed the teapot, which continued steeping on the table, reached high for the tin on the top of the refrigerator for cookies and put them on a dish. After that, all that was necessary was the teacups and a napkin. She took two linen napkins form the top drawer of the buffet and set them next to the teacups. He stood waiting until she was ready.

"You can sit here, and I'll take the other seat. Do you like milk in your tea or sugar?"

"I like it black."

She bowed her head and said, "Thank you, Lord, for this food."

He sat watching her, thinking she acted just like a child.

Before the week was out, he was convinced he should marry her. He knew she wouldn't consent to sex unless she was married. He really thought this was the best thing he had ever decided to do. *It could help me go straight. Having a wife with the appearance of a young child could be exactly what I need. All I have to do is train her the way I want her to be. Quiet, never talk unless addressed. And most of all, she must do as I say.*

She truly was naive and was unaware of his plans. She stood at his door and knocked.

"Why, hello, what brings you here today?"

"I thought you would go to church with me this Sunday. Would you?"

"Which church do you go to?"

"I go to the Baptist Church in Hessel, is that okay?"

"Sure, what time?"

"The service starts at 11:00 a.m., so can you drive? I don't have a car."

"Of course, I'd be glad to drive you."

Right into my hands, sweetheart. As gullible as you are, you're going to be easy, as easy as putting bait on my hook.

"See you tomorrow morning, around half past ten."

He couldn't believe his eyes when he saw her walking across the yard from her home to his. He smiled, while he appraised her dress, shoes, and total appearance. She did look just like a little girl all dressed up for church.

On the other hand, she looked at him repulsed. His shirt comprised of two colors that conflicted and hurt the eyes to look at. *Good grief,* she thought, *at least it's clean.*

He stood holding the passenger door open for her; she smiled and jumped into his 1952 Ford. The short three and a half mile ride to the church remained quiet and slightly solemn. She held her Bible tightly in her hands. The truck stopped, and he rushed to open the door for her again. She stepped out feeling like a princess. She had never been treated this way before. After church, he took her out to dinner. It was stuffed flounder, with all the trimmings. Everything was delicious, even the warm cherry pie with a scoop of vanilla ice cream. Later he asked her if she wanted to go for a ride.

She answered, "Yes," smiling like a child.

They rode west of town here and there. He showed her homes that were something she knew she would never ever live in, as they were far more expensive than her income would ever afford. Eventually they were on Simmons Road. As they curved through the sandy roads, the truck was sliding sideways and made her slightly nervous. On the one curve, he stopped and said, "Do you know what this spot is?"

"No. I have never been here before," she answered.

"This is where that Adams girl was found murdered." She looked across at the old farmhouse and was sure she saw a movement in the upstairs window.

"Does anyone live over there?"

"Not for years, it has been vacant and is falling apart, even the barn is decadent."

He continued to drive farther up the road, around a curve, and slowed down to show her where they found the dead girl's schoolbag. "This is where they found the schoolbag."

"How far is this to our home?" she asked.

"Don't you worry your little head, baby doll."

"Why did you call me that?"

"Because you remind me of a baby doll, you're so small and cuddly."

She blushed and looked out the truck window shyly.

Soon they were on their way home. They had taken so many curves, she was lost and was sure she would never find this spot again. That movement in the window stayed in her thoughts long after she went home, and even later when she went to bed.

She slept restlessly.

One fine day, a couple of weeks later, she received a letter in the mail. She saw immediately it was from her older brother Arnold. She glanced across the way toward her neighbors' house. He was not home. Probably still at the woods cutting.

In the letter she read, as she sat out front on a green metal lawn chair, that her brother Arnold and his wife, Dorothy, were coming up to get her and the family car. The cottage would be sold and divided between the two siblings. However, the car belonged to Arnold since he was the one who provided it for their parents. He had asked for the key when her father died, so the car sat there ever since.

Her news would be kept secret. She had a gut feeling that she should not say a thing to anyone about it. She felt she could not tell him.

Her brother Arnold planned to be up the first day of June, which would give her time to get things packed. It also would give her ample time to get the home cleaned up and ready for sale.

That weekend, her neighbor asked her to attend church with him again.

"Same one?" she asked.

"Yes, you liked it, didn't you?"

"It was fine." She loved the grand piano. And the lady, Genevieve, could make it sing, while the most beautiful chords rolled out into the sanctuary making it alive with the Holy Spirit. Pastor Jacobs usually preached a great sermon. The sermon lesson left her refueled for the week to come.

Her answer was submissive. He liked that.

After church, he decided to drive to St. Ignace, taking the scenic route through the pines and cedars, old trails that were melted away from the winter's snow. Finally, they came out on the old Mackinaw Trail just south of the Pine River near Rudyard.

The air was fresh with the smell of new grass, cedar, and the buzz of bees and other insects. After a few curves, she could see through the opening of the pines, a glimpse of Lake Huron. Soon they were circling and went over the Pine River once again, along the shoreline, going at a slower pace. Many of the restaurants were full with tourists and the after-church members. Eventually, they came to the hotel restaurant, where it appeared there was some room for extra customers.

They found a seat near one of the front lace curtained windows, where the warmth of the noonday sun streamed in, and they could easily see across to Mackinaw Island. Today was special, he had told her. It gave a quick surge of excitement in her body.

"Today, I'm ordering a plate of whitefish, with those french fries and coleslaw," he told her. "You know they serve homemade biscuits here on Sunday also?"

"That sounds like something I would like. I will order what you are having."

Again he was pleased that she was agreeable. He smiled inside.

They drank Eight O'clock brand coffee while they waited for the meal. The place was packed, so they knew it would be a while for the meal to be served. As they waited, they watched the automobiles as they passed. In the water beyond the shore, they saw a ferryboat take tourists across to the island, soon another one returned with tourists who spent the morning there.

A few minutes later, their steaming plates arrived, which looked delicious. It was even garnished with a sprig of fresh parsley. A small ceramic dish held tartar sauce for the fish. She had never seen the likes of this plate. It was a special day after all.

Later they drove a different way home, taking the sand roads here, there, until she recognized they were near the old rundown farmhouse. She looked immediately up to the window on the second floor and gasped. A girl stood in the window. She looked young, around ten to twelve years old. Then she disappeared as quickly as she appeared. He didn't seem to notice, as his gaze was fixed on the spot to the right where the crime took place. It had been more than a year ago, almost two, yet it was like yesterday to him, and he wanted to experience another like that one was. It was so good for him. He ached for the desire and fulfillment that his last victim gave him. He ached to feel the seduction, the forced play with his little "baby doll."

The next day, around one in the afternoon, a car drove into her driveway. She knew right away that it was her brother Arnold and his wife, Dorothy. They sat for a moment taking in the view of the entire yard and dwelling. They noticed the small pale-blue color storage shed in the back. The grass needed mowing, which would help sell the place. The shack, Arnold called it, needed a new coat of paint.

"We'll have it done by the real estate agent. He can hire someone to paint the cottage and the shed the same color. That should add a couple hundred dollars to the sale. Let's go in."

They noticed the shade swing back, so they knew she was inside waiting.

She answered the door, peeking out timidly.

"Hey, Sarah, aren't you going to ask us in?" her brother asked.

She swung the door wide and stepped back, which allowed them to enter the tiny kitchen. The couple stood and looked all around the home with a surprised expression, for Sarah had cleaned it to perfection.

"This looks really nice and ready for anyone to move into. Hurry, Sarah, we need to catch the ferry back to Lower Michigan and on home before it becomes too late."

Tears sprung into her eyes, but she concealed them by turning to get her few belongings in the bedroom. Ten minutes later, they were down the road and on their way. Arnold drove the Pontiac, and Sarah rode with Dorothy in their black Ford sedan.

* * * * *

That evening, he returned home tired after a long day working in the woods. He threw his hat on the table and took a long drink from the well. He pumped the bucket full of fresh water and carried it in to the sink counter. He looked out the window in her direction to find that the car was gone. Dumbfounded, he wondered where she went.

He rested a minute before he went out to get the mail. There was just junk mail, so he returned to the house via Sarah's yard. He immediately noticed two sets of tire tracks, one larger than the other, and overlapping the first. Her old man's car was gone.

She had company. I wonder who. No one ever comes here. Strange that she never mentioned having friends or relatives. I thought she was alone without anyone to answer to. Damn. He threw the junk mail on the ground and stomped on it. Then he looked around to see if anyone saw him. Slowly he reached down and picked it up. When he entered the cottage, he threw the paper in the stove. He would light it to make supper later.

He was so angry, he went out back and began splitting the cut logs and stacked the pieces against the cabin. After an hour, he was calmed down and ready to fix dinner.

* * * * *

George sat impatiently in the waiting room of the hospital. He couldn't hear anything from the other room. He stood up several times, paced back and forth, and finally sat down. Suddenly he heard Maria's shout, "Oh, help!" Then one of the nurses told Maria, "Bear down, Maria, the baby is ready to be born."

Next he heard Maria, "Okay, I'm doing it, is it..." Then silence. A moment later, he heard a slap and a loud cry from a newborn.

The door opened to the waiting room. "Come in, George, your son is born, and Maria is fine."

Maria held little George Junior in her arms, smiling. She weakly held him out to George. A big smile crossed his face as he reached for his namesake and held him close. He reached for his wife and gave her a very proud hug.

"This is one of the happiest moments in my life, Maria. Are you feeling okay?"

"I'm a little tired, but I'm going to be fine as soon as I get a nap." She took the baby and gave him her nipple, while George watched his son, George, receive his first meal.

* * * * *

A week later after, Sarah had left without one word to Matt, the woodsman found a letter in the mailbox from Sarah. It was thick, four pages in all. She wrote that she was making a new life near her brother. She stayed with a man who had four children and had recently lost his wife to pneumonia. He was a farmer and needed her to be there to take care of him and the children. As he read, he could hear her say, "Their names are Justin, Jerry, Jane, and James, she wrote. I cook, clean house, wash clothes, do the weekly grocery shopping, and then I can spend Sunday with my brother Arnold and his wife, Dorothy."

He wadded up the letter and threw it across the room. "I'm foiled again!" he screamed. Then he became so angry, he picked the wadded letter, threw it down, and stomped on it several times. The door slammed as he pushed his way outdoors, pulled on his hair, and roared like a wounded animal.

Then he realized he needed the letter to write back to her. He needed to tell her he wanted her to come back, live with him, and even marry him if she would. He couldn't bear the worrisome fact that she may fall in love with the single farmer and his four children. He screwed his face into an ugly look as he thought of this ever happening. He went back in the house to search for the letter, which had lodged under his couch, and gently straightened it out to retrieve the address he so longed to have. Sarah, he noted her name was Sarah Johnson, who lived in North Branch, Michigan. The address was in care of Arnold Johnson. That bastard, it's his entire fault. If she has been with the farmer before I get her, I'll never forgive her. Then a smile swiftly replaced his disfigured, nasty look, as he sweetly smiled to himself and began writing the persuasive letter back to her.

Sarah read his letter a few days later. It read, "Sarah, my baby doll, I need you here more than that man, the farmer with four children, does. I have missed you terribly. I haven't slept well since you left. I've lost weight, and all I think of is you, my sweet baby doll. Will you please return to me and marry me? I can't be here alone, after the wonderful times we have had together. I have enclosed enough money for you to take a bus to Mackinac City. Wait for me there. I will come across on the Big Chief to get you. Just let me know when and what day." He signed it, "Your man."

It was Sunday when she finally received the letter. Her brother, Arnold, watched as his wife, Dorothy, gave it to her after church. Surprisingly he hadn't kept it from her. Actually, it was Dorothy who saved it for Sarah. Arnold was just as surprised as Sarah was to see a letter for her. Her curiosity was answered when she saw it was from him. She ran to her bedroom to read it.

Her heart was filled with joy as she read his true wishes. She knew she loved him immediately and wanted to join him right away. She wrote back that she would take the bus from North Branch, transfer at Saginaw, and take the route to Mackinac City, early Saturday morning. This would give the farmer, Don Williams, time to find a new governess. She also would have one more pay week for extra spending, to cover her needs.

I've worked hard for this one. It better be worth my investment, he thought. *Most men just get relief by going to a special place and pay for what they want. But there are consequences that could ruin oneself for life. I want it the way I direct it. She better do just as I say or it's curtains for her.*

He worked diligently all that week. Friday, he took a bath one day early, so he could leave before dawn on Saturday. The drive to St. Ignace took an hour, when he reached town he went to the court house to see what he would have to do to get married that day. He found he couldn't get married right away, so he went to see his friend, a shady creature, who did anything for money. He was a lawyer by trade. For the right amount of money, he was willing to perform a fake marriage well enough, even the pope would believe him. He knew he could convince Sarah that she truly was married to him. He hated to spend the money, but it would cost as much if he had to return in the suggested time legally. Taking him away from his work in the woods was money, after all, so now he waited for the ferry to get across to Mackinac City.

Finally, the ferry came to shore at the edge of Mackinac City. He searched for Sarah. He looked up and down the board sidewalk along the depot landing. The bus had long gone, according to the teller. He couldn't see her anywhere. *Did she change her mind? Keep my money? That bitch. Oh, there she is, sitting down on the side bench.* A feeling of relief changed his mood.

"Sarah, I looked all over for you, so glad to see you." Smiling, he gave her a brief hug. "Hurry, we must return with the ferry in order to reach the marriage justice on time."

She reached to kiss him, thinking it was appropriate, but he had already turned toward the ferry.

The unsteady rolling of the waves made her stomach churn. By the time they finally reached St. Ignace, she was weak on her feet and sick to her stomach. She obediently followed him to his truck, which was familiar to her by now, got in, and rode silently to the office of the man who would make them man and wife.

They were greeted by a man fully dressed in a three-piece dress suit. His hair slicked back, he wore a pair of spectacles on the bridge of his nose, and wore a smile on his greedy lips.

"This is Thomas Crane, esquire. He will perform the ceremony." He had already told Tom to use the pseudo name Matt Dillon in place of his own real name, which was Clarence Grimshaw.

"Yes, my dear, you can stand here, and, err, Matt, you stand here."

Thomas Crane cleared his throat, and in his very professional and most sincere voice began his act. "On this day, with the fact that these two wish to come together and become one in marriage, and with the power invested in me, before God and the birds that sing outdoors, I now pronounce you man and wife," he grimaced at his fake words. *Hokey, but it will work*, he thought. "You may kiss the bride."

He reached for her, and she grabbed her stomach and said, "Where is the bathroom?" She ran in that direction and slammed the door. The two could hear Sarah vomit.

"Is she pregnant?" Thomas Crane asked.

"No, she is not," he answered indignantly. "She better not be."

Sarah finally came out red in the face and apologetic.

She reached for him, however, he reached in his hind pocket for his billfold, gave Crane, esquire, a twenty-dollar bill. He rushed her out the door and back into the truck.

It was dark by the time they reached the sandy road to his home. She waited for him to carry her over the threshold; however, he never gave it a thought. Humbly, she followed in and waited for his next move.

"Are you hungry?" he asked her.

"Not really."

"Then let's go to bed. Morning will come soon enough."

They undressed in the dark. He wanted to see her, but she was shy. Finally he turned on the bedroom light. "I want to see you." He threw her on the bed and became rough with her. She became scared and fought him. He loved it. She struggled through the whole act, which made him ecstatic. A strong libido created instant desire that couldn't be denied. While he chewed on her neck, a growling sound came from his throat. Then the overwhelming release consumed him.

He rolled off her. Sarah heard him snore within a minute.

She lay silent for a long time. She was confused and ached with physical and mental pain.

The next day was usual. He got up, ate breakfast of gruel, and toast, then left for work. She cleaned herself first and dressed ready to clean the home. Later while she was working, she became curious enough to dig into his personal things. As she dug, she heard him enter the house, so she quickly entered the kitchen to greet him.

"What were you doing in there?"

"I made the bed and cleaned up a little."

"Remember, it's my bed. Come sit here by me on the couch. I have a few laws for you to follow. Number one, never touch my things."

"Yes, Matt."

"Second, don't call me Matt. You say *sir*."

"Yes, sir."

"Never ask questions about my past." He looked closely into her eyes, reached out, and held her head with both hands. "I know I'm older than you, but age doesn't matter. I also don't want you to make contact with your brother again, understand? I want you for my own."

This made her happy. She was made to feel loved and wanted.

"I came back because this is Sunday, and we should go to church."

"Yes, sir."

Later that evening, he led her to the bedroom, threw her on the bed, and handled her the way he did the night before. She fought again, and he had his way. He laughed aloud so she realized he liked it. That was enough for her. To please him was the most important thing for her. She didn't question his actions at all.

It was still daylight, yet he snored loudly and slept the night through till dawn.

A week passed with what seemed like a repetitive performance each day. She truly wanted to feel as good as he did, but it wouldn't happen. Much as she tried to relax, take it as it went, nothing happened, other than she felt good because he was happy. She made up her mind to cling to him and see if this was the solution.

He was home after a long day. He was fed, he cleaned up, and she knew that soon he would want to retire for the evening. She prolonged this until he finally said, "Let's go to bed."

"Already?" she asked.

"Remember, don't ask me, we're going when I say."

"Yes, sir," she silently smiled.

He threw her down, ripped off her nightgown, and began. She clung to him as she had never done before, which made him stop.

"Fight me."

"Why?"

"Because I said so, baby doll."

She really didn't want to do what he commanded, however, she fought.

Soon a month went by. It was midsummer, the weather that day was beautiful, and she finally was enjoying flowers in her garden. He came home slightly early that day. As she looked, she saw him stop at the mailbox, he shoved a letter in his pocket, then drove into the yard. He seemed upset.

"What are you doing digging in the mud like a pig? I don't want you to get all dirty. You're my baby doll, understand?"

"Yes, sir."

"Go in and clean up." He pointed with a Hitler-like sternness toward the backdoor. All he needed was a square mustache to fill the similarity.

A month of uncertain emotions and wondering what she had done to have a life in this condition. She asked herself if this was what a marriage was like. She had always thought it would be a show of love, a gentle smile, and lots of sharing.

Each day seemed the same and nothing changed. She half thought she should write to her brother for answers. But she feared her brother would say she had made the decision to marry the woodsman, so she should stay and quit complaining to him. She knew there was no way out. She would have to keep saying, "Yes, sir," and do as he wished. That's what a wife's role was, to be submissive.

Four months later, she was just finishing her chores when he arrived home. He called her a filthy mess. "Go and clean yourself up, slut."

She went into the bathroom, started the water for a bath, and began undressing. She could hear the noise of him as he rattled the pans and dishes. He must be getting dinner fixed. She smiled as she sat in the tub, cleaned up, dried off, and came back into the kitchen bare naked.

He ran to her, carried her into the bedroom, and raised his hand high. As he began to slap her, he screamed, "Don't ever, ever come out of the bathroom undressed again!" He continued to slap her repeatedly until she began to scream. He left the room and came back. He looked at her lying there, she held back the tears and just looked. He undressed. He slowly crawled on the bed, grabbed her, and began doing what she called his relief act. She didn't fight or cling to him. He began to slam her with his fist, thinking she would fight, but she didn't. Suddenly he began to choke her, she still didn't fight. This made him become angry, and he continued squeezing tighter and tighter until her entire body went limp. He continued slamming into her with his body, in the husbandly way that he did. He let out a cry of relief and lay on top of her, exhausted.

For an hour, he lay beside her. *Now what do I do? Serves her right, she must have written to him. I told her not to. What if she didn't write her brother? It was too late even if she didn't. She asked for it, the slut. She caused me to break her neck. Oh, whatever, she wasn't the first one.*

He rolled over, turned his back to her, and fell soundly to sleep.

Two days later, he came home and realized there was a terrible stench in the house. He went back outdoors, took a shovel out of the shed. He looked both ways down the road to see if anything or anyone was near. He went across and behind her old home that was sold to tourist who had not been there, to his knowledge, yet. He picked a spot in the backyard behind the small shed where there were very few stones and mostly sand. He dug a grave the size of her tiny body. It began to get dark, so even though the hole was shallow, he decided it was deep enough to bury her, once and for all. Get rid of her. However, he decided to use her once more before he buried her.

Fifteen minutes later, just before dark, he walked out to the road and listened. No sound was heard either way in his deserted area. He was in the clear.

He went back in the house and wrapped her in his sheet, from his bed, and threw her over his shoulder. When he reached the cupboard, he grabbed the bag of lye, and carried her to the grave site. He stopped and listened once again, for any noise of someone coming. The night was perfectly still. He flipped her to the ground, took the shovel to place her correctly, so he could easily shovel the dirt at the best vantage point, enabling him to do it precisely correct. He picked up the bag of lye and slowly poured all around and over her head. *No one would know who the corpse was, as the lye would eat away all signs of flesh and hair.* When he finished, he took the back of the shovel and packed the sand down. He turned and never looked back to that spot again.

Chapter Six
A Discovery

Another month passed, it was nearing the first frost of the fall season. Farmers were gathering the last cutting of hay for the winter. Women were canning tomatoes and digging potatoes, making pickles in crocks, drying seeds, garlic, and onions hung in a rope from the storage beam in their sheds or barns. Soon the last mowing would succumb to the frost and the mowers could be cleaned, oiled, and stored for the winter. The remaining months would include picking dry corn from the fields for grain, stored in cribs, and use as needed. They would take it to the gristmill, a load at a time, have it ground and bagged for the cattle, pigs, and chickens.

Don Williams walked in to see George early one morning. He shook George's hand and started by asking about the new baby at his home. "How's your new son, George? Susie? And your wife, how is she?"

"Just fine. George, my son, is doing fine and is six months old now. Little Susie loves to help mommy with him."

"I saw her in the news office when I entered. Susie will be back to school soon. I suppose Maria will bring little George in with her each day."

"Yes, the children spent the summer here unless they went with Fred, my brother, and his new wife, Penny, to the lake or wherever they planned for them that day." He paused. "Don, I know you aren't here for small talk, what brings you here today?"

"It's a long story. Do you have the time? I didn't bring my bed roll, so I'll try to finish before suppertime."

George chuckled. "I'm listening."

"It all started about a couple weeks ago. My dog Rex would leave, then after a while, he would return with a bone to chew on. Within a week, he had a pile of them. I didn't think much about this. Deer carcasses often are a common thing in the woods, and he always has brought them home from time to time. Once he dragged the whole thing, including the hide home. Stink, did it ever. I hollered at him and took it out behind the barn and unloaded the manure on top of it. He didn't bother trying to dig it out again.

"The bones he brought, after I looked closely were smaller, possibly from a fawn, even a pig, so I still wasn't suspicious of anything else, but that the dog was doing what dogs do. Yesterday, he brought home a skull, human skull."

George sat upright in his chair. "What?" he said loudly. Even Maria heard George with the doors closed.

"Not a big one, but definitely a human skull."

"Where is it?"

"It's out in the truck, in a burlap bag."

"Please go get it and bring it in here where I can take a close look at it."

Don Williams returned with a burlap bag hanging from one of his strong big hands. He was a redhead with a ruddy complexion. His height was near six feet. He had the stature of a strong man who could handle his share of farm work. He wore a sweat-stained straw hat which sat atop his head. When he took it off, his forehead was divided with tan and white where the hat hid the sunrays after a season of long days in the field.

George had cleared his desk and laid old newspapers down for Mr. Williams to place the skull. They both examined the skull, without touching it with their bare hands. George took out his camera and flash cubes. He loaded the camera and took shots of each side. They used rubber gloves to keep from touching it. It appeared to be intact. George looked at Mr. Williams and said, "Thank you for bringing this in for me. I also wish to come out tomorrow morning. Maybe we can follow Rex to his treasure spot. I will take the skull in to St. Ignace to the Mackinaw County Sheriff office right away this afternoon. From there, it will be examined by the coroner. I'll be out in the morning, Don, about eight o'clock?"

"That'll be fine, George. See you then."

George spent the remaining day traveling to St. Ignace, where he not only took the skull to the county sheriff's office but inquired if there were any reports of a missing person in the last month or so. He thought about the cold case that hadn't been solved twenty-four months ago. He remembered the death of the little Adams girl, and how he had not been able to get any leads to solve it. It haunted him for these past two years, and still nothing surfaced to help his search for the sociopath running loose. He wondered if there could be a connection with this skull or were there more corpses somewhere buried in no man's land waiting to be discovered. He detoured out past the old Miller farm on his way home. He looked forlornly at the discovery spot, aching to know the secret that lay there. The decadent farm remained the same, with more wear in the past two years. He glanced to the second-story window where he believed he saw a girl standing there. It disappeared as fast as it appeared. Was it his imagination? Was it her? Was it the Adams girl? Would she remain there until he solved the crime? Would she wait until there was closure and peace for her?

He drove slowly away, with a heavy heart. *Soon, little girl, I can feel it in my heart. Soon, I will find your killer.*

* * * * *

Many would call him a sociopath; he didn't mix with others even when he worked, and at this point, his actions would be considered to be a psychopath. His thought pattern was beyond the realm of reality. George was sure it was someone who simply did his job and returned home. Possibly only went to shop for his supplies every few months. Lived off the land and the few staples he would need to survive. George thought of one Pierre Bouchard, who fit that description, but it was said he had moved down the line and had not been seen for more than a couple of years. However, Pierre did go to the Cedarville Bar every so often. This guy obviously didn't drink, kept to himself, and had just one vice. It was little girls for sure. George suspected this wasn't the first because he covered his tracks quite well. He had become a pro at it.

The next morning, George headed out to the Williams's place. It was located around a curve and up against a large plot of woods.

Williams farmed some and worked at the quarry during the week on the afternoon shift.

George drove up the drive to discover Don near his machine shed. He appeared to be repairing a seed drill. "Howdy, George, you know John Deere builds a great drill, but the parts go out because of the strength of the fertilizer, eats right through them."

"They are shot, Don, that fertilizer sure did eat the downspouts away. Is the dog around?"

"He was here just a couple minutes ago, there he goes. We'll give him a few minutes, then we'll follow." Don's gaze spotted Rex across the field headed toward the woods. Don wiped the grease off his hands he had used to cover the drill parts on an old rag.

They followed Rex across and through the woods to the other road. Rex wasn't in a hurry, to the relief of the two men. The dog sniffed here and there wandering all around. Maybe he was hoping to find food closer to home. Rex crossed that road and reentered another forest of trees. They followed him as he sniffed here and there, under stumps, near tree roots, and moss piles. Finally he came out of the woods and strolled across a field toward a small cabin and shed.

"Hold on, Don," George said in a quiet voice. "Let's see if he digs for a bone here or goes on farther." He held his hand out to stop Don from proceeding. They stood and waited, watching from the woods edge. The cabin was over a football field's length away. There was a road and one more dwelling on this stretch of road, across and over a few yards. That cabin was small also with a shed, with a board fence around it.

Sure enough, Rex sniffed around the area. When he began digging, George motioned for Don to leave back through the woods. It was two miles back to the Williams's place. George decided it would be better if the dog didn't see them. So a head start back would be the best decision.

After they were out of earshot, George said, "We will have to compare this bone to the ones he has brought back before. He did seem to know exactly where he was going."

"I'll have to agree with you, George," Don answered then continued, "so you will go over there to look for more clues?"

"Yes, right away, while it is fresh and the hole is open. I'll need a shovel and a sack to put any evidence in it. I'll need my camera, all which is in my trunk."

"I'd love to go with you, but I have to get ready for work, George."

"That's okay, you have been a great help already. I'll call in for a deputy from St. Ignace. Could I use your phone?"

"Sure."

They were finally out of the woods and walking across the field toward the Williams's place by this time. It would be a matter of ten minutes before they would reach the house.

"The phone is on the wall there by the kitchen table. I'll go in and clean up," Don pointed at it as he headed to the bathroom.

* * * * *

Deputy Paquin drove up to the cabin on the sandy road near the place where the bones were discovered by the dog. George had waited for nearly an hour for his arrival, making it a little later in the afternoon. He had his shovel out and a couple of bags ready to go in back of the shed. He had taken pictures while he waited but would need it to take more as they dug and discovered anything else in the hole.

Paquin got out, took a shovel out of his trunk, and they both headed out where George pointed. Paquin shook his hand, "What do we have here, George, whatever else comes with the skull?"

"I suspect so, Deputy Paquin, and I'm hoping to find some clue to tell us who this body is. So far the dog has brought home ribs and then the skull. What I'm thinking is, we'll find the arms, torso, hands, legs, and feet. Maybe we'll find clothing or anything that will help the investigation."

"Normally you would need a pick axe, so I brought one, but I see this ground is all sand, so I don't think we'll need it," the deputy said.

They strolled through the tall weeds and grass to the backyard behind the small storage shed. George began by digging a square trench around the hole where the dog, Rex, had been digging.

This would avoid destroying evidence. Next the two carefully dug inward toward the hole, throwing the sand away from it.

An hour of digging caused them to stop and take off their outer shirt.

"Hey, I found something. It's a bone, another rib." Paquin said, elated. He carefully put it in one of the bags. After a few more minutes another discovery was found.

"Look at this!" George exclaimed. "Looks like a sheet. Help me, we need to try to keep it in one piece, and try to protect any evidence here, like stains or blood on it." The stench of the body was putrid.

"Gently, dig gently." George slipped fresh rubber gloves on and began digging gently with his hands brushing the sand away from the body wrapped in a sheet."

"Whoever did this definitely wanted to keep anyone from knowing who the person was."

"I can call in on my car radio, or at least try. With all the wooded areas between here and St. Ignace, it may be impossible to get through. Anyway we'll try to get a hearse out here. Someone isn't going to like this job."

"Apparently, the dog cleaned all the flesh off the skull before bringing it home. This is a half gone and rank body. I don't envy his job either."

"Look here, Paquin, the sheet appears to have decayed away along the top edge down about a foot. Strange that only that part was rotted away. I'm taking a sample of the sand around this area and an additional one at the lower part of the grave for comparison and testing."

"Good idea, George, I think you have something to go on. Yep, you're on to something."

George kept digging looking for evidence to see if it was female or male, while Paquin called in to the sheriff's office.

"They're sending Drake out. He's on his way. Keep digging?"

"Yup, we can look for jewelry, keys, anything that may be a part of this body. Since there wasn't any clothing on the corpse, and it was wrapped in a sheet, it appears as though it may have been a sex crime since the body is bare. The coroner will be able to find this for us."

The men had been shaking the dirt off as they sifted through the closer sand, searching for anything that might connect to this discovery. Periodically, they would hear a clinking noise to discover it was a pebble or a small rock. Suddenly George heard a duller sound against his shovel while he sifted the dirt off his shovel. The item was covered with wet sand, so he brushed it off to discover a keychain with the letter S on it. He dropped it into a small evidence bag and grinned to himself. *One step closer*, he thought. *But this keychain could have been here in the sand for a long time, even before the body was buried.*

George knew it would be late before he would return home this day. However, Maria always understood and kept things on an even keel. Feed the children, put them to bed, save prime time for him when he finally did return. She always wanted to know about his day, but always kept from asking. It was up to him if he could or would share anything with her. Understanding was her middle name.

The hearse drove up in the yard and around to the back shed. Paquin directed Drake when he heard him driving up the road.

The job of getting the half-rotted body out and on the stretcher was tedious, but it helped to have three working on it. They dug on a slope from the ground level, and then lay the stretcher up against the body, so as to hardly keep from touching it. Next they rolled it over onto the stretcher, covered it with an extra sheet from the hearse, and strapped it down for travel.

"This one's ripe," Drake said, holding his kerchief to his nose. "It's a rare day to get one like this."

"Drake, we don't envy you this job. I'll check back with you after discovery. I did find a keychain, and that's all I have to go on until I hear from you." George waved at him as he drove off.

Paquin and George walked to their cars, removed their rubber gloves, and wiped their hands off with grass along the roads edge and went their different way toward home.

George looked over at the fenced-in cabin as he drove off. The light was on in the cabin. A rusty 52 Ford was parked next to the side door. The driver had backed in, so George could see the grill with a chrome V-8 in it. He pulled off the road and knocked at the door. No answer. He knocked again.

"How can I help you, Officer?" A tall man stood almost next to him.

"Hello," a startled George responded. "My name's George Kaughman. I'd like to ask you a few questions."

"Well, what is it? Is there a law against burying potato peelings in the garden after dark?" He laughed.

"No. Have you seen anyone around here lately?"

"Would you like to step in out of the dark?" He gestured to the door, walked in, and George followed. He continued by answering, "No, just that pesky dog. I chased him away a couple times. He hung at my door step. I don't like dogs. And just today I saw you and that other guy. Then the other long car, like a hearse, pulled all the way back there. What's going on over there anyway?"

"It's a long story, and all I need to do is ask you a few more questions. What about any other people, do you see many of them?"

"I work all the time, no, I haven't seen any."

"Does someone live across the way in that cabin?"

"No."

"Do you know who owns it?"

"No."

"Thanks." George looked at him and wondered who he was. He had never seen him before. He noticed the small home was immaculately clean. This man had a feather duster stuck in his rear pocket, which made George think he was cleaning while his supper cooked.

"Lived here long?"

"Ten years."

"What's your name?"

"Matthew Dillon."

"Okay, Matthew, thank you. If you do recall anything, please call me. The fact is the dog found a body buried out back of the next-door home." George handed him his card. George turned and stepped out of the house into the darkness. He backed out of Matt's drive and drove toward home. George thought he would have shaken his hand, but Matt's hand looked dirty. It was the lack of reaction from Matt that made George wonder. It was almost indifferent. "That's a good reason as any to not like dogs. How would you like being eaten one meal at a time after you were dead?" Matt stared straight ahead with no reaction whatever. George shook his head and left.

Later at his office, George stopped for a minute and set the pen down, pausing to think. Up to this point, he had related all that took place that day from the beginning at Don Williams's home, the trek through the two miles of woods, discovery of the dog's hidden treasure of bones and the body. Then later at the neighbor's home, James Madison, or Matthew Dillon, who seemed to be a congenial individual. He completed his narration on paper as the day came to an end and set down his ink pen.

After a moment, he looked back to the page when he picked up his pen and continued to write, "A couple things in question is that the sheet was worn away at the top where the head was wrapped. There was no sign of hair in the sand, nor in the vicinity of the buried body. The body was nude, even in the decayed state there should have been some trace of clothing. Apparently it couldn't have been there very long. Being in a shallow grave, the dog probably wasn't the only carnivorous animal tearing away on the carcass. I have to commend Don Williams for his quick response in wondering where the bones came from. Without his coming into the office yesterday, I would have never found the body. For now I am waiting for a report from the coroner's office to further investigate who this person was. End of entry for this date."

George looked at the old Ingram clock that hung across him on the wall that ticked as the pendulum swung. The time was almost eight-thirty. It was time for him to head home, clear his mind of the stupefying, puzzling discovery of the day, and spend a few minutes with Maria before retiring for the day. Tomorrow would be a new beginning.

The next day began with thoughts about a few more things that happened the day before. As he did his routine chores, he continued to think. Breakfast was routine. Maria sent Susie off to school. She left for the office with little George in her vehicle, while George followed in his county patrol car.

Arriving at the office, he took out his journal and began to write. "The person, James Madison, is a tall man with a receding hairline. He has dark-brown curly hair and long sideburns, dark eyes, and a slim body build. He appears to be around forty-four to forty-seven years of age. His teeth are false. He keeps a clean, shaved face. His feet are wide and long, possibly size twelve. He drives an early rusty '50s Ford pickup truck. His dwelling is small but clean. There are curtains dividing the bedroom from the remaining part of the home also the bathroom. This may indicate his income could be meager. He stated he worked in the woods." George set the pen back in the ink well. He leaned back in his swivel desk chair; he thought about what his next step would be. He could ask around about this guy, but there wasn't anything leading him to need to. He didn't appear to be the kind of person who could be a sociopath nor a psychopath. He actually acted very normal in fact. George read his entry again and noticed he had written James Madison, erased it, and replaced the name as Matt Dillon. He stored the entry book in the locked drawer in his desk.

Abruptly, a hunch entered George's mind. He swung around off the chair, grabbed his jacket, and went over to the post office. "Good morning, Shelia, do you have a minute for a couple questions?"

"Sure, George, I can always take a break. Question away."

"I'm wondering about a man by the name of James Madison, I mean, Matt Dillon. Do you have him on your mail route?"

"Let me see, what road does he live on?"

"Supposedly he lives on the North Road."

"North Road, not to my knowledge. How long has he lived there?"

"I heard around ten years."

"No mail goes on the North Road. There are only two homes on that road. The first one had a couple live there, but they died suddenly and no one has heard from their family since. The second one had a man and his daughter living there, but he died and she moved away. It was sold to someone from Chicago, but no one has ever seen the buyer either. Wait a minute, there was a letter sent out that way about two months ago. The mail carrier dropped it off, but there has not been any mail sent back out since then."

"Do you remember who the letter was sent to?"

"A woman, but I don't recall her name."

Chapter Seven
How It Happened

He craved for sexual satisfaction, just like he wanted with the two "baby dolls" he had killed. His whole body ached for more. Over three months had passed since his last pleasure.

Leaving from the woods, he noticed a sweet little thing, walking toward the next road where there was a single farm about a half mile to the west. He slowed his truck down, rolled down the window, and asked, "Hello there, are you lost?"

"No, I just got off the bus and am headed for home over there." She pointed at an empty field and woods beyond.

"Have you ever seen a baby puppy? My dog just had them a couple days ago, and they are just so adorable. Want to see them?"

She looked toward the direction of her family farm but changed her mind and threw her schoolbag in the ditch to retrieve later. Then she jumped into the truck.

The six-mile ride to his place didn't take too long. He deliberately drove here and there so she wouldn't remember where he lived. As they rode there, he asked her, "Do you have a dog?"

"Yes, but he's getting older."

"When these are old enough, I will give you one. How's that sound?"

"Oh, I would be so happy to have one, but I'd have to ask my parents first."

"That's okay, I'm sure they will say yes."

She smiled happily as they turned down his road. Anticipation showed on her face.

He pulled into the yard and behind the cabin. "They're out here behind the shed follow me."

He took her hand and led her to the rear of the shed. "I need to stop here for a minute to get some food for the mama dog," he said, then reached for the dog food in a tin can and resumed their walk around behind.

She immediately noticed there was no dog or puppies out there. "Where are they?"

He asked her if she would like to show him what was under her skirt.

"No, I don't, please take me back home."

"I can't do that, baby doll, I want to see your other parts."

She began to run. He grabbed her and began to raise the skirt of her dress.

"No, don't," she begged.

She wasn't fighting; he wanted her to fight. He slapped her, hard. It made her mad, so she punched him in the face. This caused him to stagger backward, almost falling. "You little slut, I'll have my way with you no matter what."

"Oh, no, you won't!" she screamed as she ran away toward the road. He caught her just as she was even with his side door. He threw his long arms around her and dragged her into the house and into the bedroom, to the same spot he had finished off his wife just two months earlier. She struggled to get away, as he held her down and began to rip off her clothing. She dug into his arms, shirt, and anywhere she could grab. He laughed hysterically and jerked off her panties. Penetration caused her to scream with pain. "That's it, fight me, baby doll! That's what I want!" In spite of her struggles and twisting, he was more entranced with the thrill he experienced. She screamed again, so he held his hand down on her mouth. He kept pounding away until he finally stopped and collapsed on top of her.

His height found him with his face in the pillow, while she was below him, suffocated from the bulk of his body. He felt her limp body and knew he would have to finish her if she wasn't dead. She would tell who he was and what he did. *I could drop her in the ditch as I did the other one or just bury her like the one around two months ago.*

He went out to the shed, took out a shovel, and began digging a grave for her a few paces away from his fence, where he could bury her with sand and grass, then put his compost pile over her. It took him quite a while to get a grave deep enough. Finally, after he struggled with rocks, gravel, and grass, he was ready to go get the body. He walked into the house to find that the bed was empty. He looked under the bed, in the bathroom, kitchen, and living room. She wasn't there. He ran out to the shed to see if she was hiding there. Then retraced his footsteps toward the truck, she wasn't in the truck either. He looked at the sand for her tracks. There were some, but only one was with a shoe. *Easy to find*, he thought. He went for his flashlight and a shirt. He noticed she had left her dress. It lay on the bed. *One shoe and no clothes, she'll get cold this time of year the sun has gone down. I'll find her.*

Tracks led to the road at the end. She turned toward her home. He jumped into his truck backed out of the drive. *It's six miles, she'll never make it.* He continued but only for a short while for the tracks disappeared with nothing for him to see but tire tracks from his own truck that he made earlier. The sun had dipped into the horizon and darkness had crept in. *Was that her crying? Or was it my imagination?* He hesitated and looked one way then the other and listened for a sound again. It was the wind blowing through the pines and birch trees. *I have to find her. If she gets home, I'm dead instead of her. A rock was all it would take to stop her in her tracks. I'll leave her in the woods. That's where she probably went. Brilliant, I'm brilliant, why didn't I think of that at first?*

He entered the woods, which was his domain. He spent two-thirds of his time in the woods. The familiar smells and sounds would lead him to her via the process of elimination. If it wasn't a familiar sound, it was her.

He heard a sound coming from the road, far in the distance, someone was calling, "Anna Belle!" Again, "Anna Belle!" The vehicle stopped for a minute waiting for an answer. No sound of an answer, he held his breath in case she was between him and the truck. She would run to it and get away. He needed her to save his life. He heard the vehicle move on down the road after waiting for an answer. He paused for a while, thinking she may move again, a branch snapped, and he was sure it was her. He headed in that direction. He heard more noises rustle through the woods. "Anna Belle, come to Daddy,

I came to find you," he faked his voice. "I won't hurt you, honey, come to Daddy."

* * * * *

Anna Belle's parents were worried desperately. Anxiety filled their entire being as they crept slowly along the edge of the road and looked either way, hoping and praying that soon she would show up smiling with her beautiful face that willingly gleamed at their presence. As they reached the end of the road, they saw very little but the shadows beyond the headlights. They would search for a while longer, then go home and call Deputy George. He would know what to do.

An hour later, they drove into the farm drive. Both were despondent. They thought she was surely dead, a bear, or she may have become lost, possibly took a shortcut and was lost. She had a habit of taking the woods home, but it didn't make sense to them. They would ask the bus driver if he dropped her off at the usual spot. Meanwhile, they dialed up George.

"You say Anna Belle didn't come home from school, it's past nine now. Where do you think she could be?"

"We think she went through the woods. Sometimes she takes a shortcut."

The first thought that entered George's head was there was a killer on the loose. He reserved his thoughts and said, "Do you want me to assemble a search and rescue team then head out your way? I will have to call a few people, but I can be there within the hour. Or if you wish to keep this secret for now, I'll come out alone and search with you."

"For now, please come alone. You know how gossip grows into a mountain in a short time. I'm hoping we will find her. You and I, we can do as much as a group. If she is lost, she will hear us and come to us."

"I'll be right out." George planned for the worst, so he grabbed his camera and a couple of flashbulbs, as well as an overpowered six-battery flashlight.

* * * * *

He searched for her for several hours. It was all her fault. She should have liked it as much as he did. *My baby doll was stupid, she could have enjoyed it. I could have had her for a few days before anyone would miss her. Of course, I would have to tie her up while I was gone to work, then I would have my way with her over and over. Why are all girls stupid?* He grabbed his hat and threw it on the ground. Then he stomped on it. His fist hit the nearest tree. He howled so loud he slammed his fist into his mouth so she wouldn't hear him. By now he was filled with disgust and hating all females. Even if she was dead, he planned to spend time with her, but it wouldn't be as good. The height of his desire was when they struggled and fought. *Power, oh, the wonderful power I feel when I'm in complete control.*

Time was slipping away, and soon he would have to give up the search. He had to return to the woods the next day after work. If anyone ran into him, he would say he was squirrel hunting. The moon was out and shining through the woods, which made it easier for him to find his way across the first three hundred sixty acres of standing hardwoods to the sandy road then across and through the smaller woods of pines and cedars across the field to his truck. Then the short half-mile drive to his cabin would take him to his resting place. Of course, he still had to clean any evidence the baby doll might have left behind. *She made the mess, I didn't. It was all her fault. I can't stand women. But I love little girls.*

George and Ralph fine-tooth-combed the woods near and around their farm. Ralph's heart dropped each time he heard a snap of a branch, only to find it wasn't her. He ached to think he may never see her again. "Anna Belle was so adventuresome that I am not surprised that she didn't come home. She daydreamed all the time. Her teacher teased her into coming back to the classroom, as she would look out the window with a dreamy expression on her face. 'Join the class, what world were you in this time, Anna Belle?' she would ask her."

"Is it possible she is hiding right now, waiting to jump out at us and say, you found me? It took you long enough," George jokingly asked.

"With that girl, anything is possible. She did hide in the barn one time, didn't come out until we found her. She said she planned to sleep in the barn if we didn't come after her."

They continued searching. Soon the sun rose from the east. By dawn, both were tired and decided to head back to the farm to get some sleep and start over after a few hours rest.

George called Maria to let her know what he was doing and what they planned to do. He yawned loudly during their conversation, took his hat off, and ran his fingers through his curly blond hair.

"Honey, I'm tired, I'll check back with you before we head out again. Love you and give the children hugs and kisses for me."

"I will, sweetheart, until later."

It was noon before George and Ralph Carter headed back out to the woods looking for a child that had not come home. Martha had prepared a breakfast of bacon and eggs with homemade toast.

George put his hat on and stepped off the front porch. Ralph was right on his heels. Ralph whistled for the dog. Quick as a wink, he was at their side. Ralph held a teddy bear to his nose so he would get Anna Belle's scent, then tossed it up on the porch swing.

"That might work, we've tried everything else. We looked in vain all night." Ralph needed more sleep. He showed he was depressed and at his wits end. He and Martha had worried all night, then a short nap, and now it had been several hours since Anna Belle became missing.

"Martha told me she prayed for so long, she fell asleep with her hands in a praying position. They were still the same when she woke this morning." George made little talk to encourage Ralph.

"Martha always did give it to the Lord, but I need a little more faith to believe that strong."

"Ralph, we all do need more faith at one time or another in our lives," George replied. "The thing is we never know God's will, and we have to accept it, no matter if it's what we want or not."

The woods were huge, covering a three hundred sixty acre square. Early frost had colored the leaves on the soft maples and oak trees. Some of the leaves were falling gently to the ground. The sun shined though the gaps between the trees making the ground warm where the leaves had fallen. The dog ran ahead of the two men, his tail swinging in a circle, as he sailed through the woods. He was easily recognizable with all the action from his tail and jumps. Over the lower fallen logs, here and there from one opening to another between trees.

Suddenly he stopped, sniffed at a fallen log, actually a fallen tree that had rotted and hollowed out. Moss had grown over it, which told it had been down for more than one year. He sniffed and began barking loudly. The men stopped and looked in that direction.

"He's spotted something, could be an animal, too early for a bear, but it looks like something is in that hollow tree." They cautiously reached into the tree, where they noticed moss everywhere. It fell off a body. The dog barked and dug at the moss to uncover the body.

"Step back, Rover, let's see what it is," George said to the dog.

"My gawd," he exclaimed, as he staggered to the ground. He shook his head to come back to reality, the life had drained from his face leaving it white.

George dragged Anna Belle gently form the log. He put his head close to her mouth to see if she was breathing. Then he felt her pulse with his fingers at the throat.

"Just a weak pulse, Ralph. She's alive, but just barely. Give me a hand here, you hold her in a sitting position while I put this coat around her. She feels very cold. If we rub her, it may bring some life into her."

George gave her his coat, while Ralph rubbed her hands, legs that were exposed to the cold, and took one of his socks off for her beaten, bloody foot.

"We need to get her home. She needs to get to the hospital as quickly as possible."

George gently cradled Anna Belle into his strong arms, and the two men hurried back through the woods to the Carter farm.

Anna Belle was unconscious. She didn't even moan when she was lifted to George's arms. Her body hung lifeless without movement.

George feared it was too late but silently prayed she would come around soon. It was less than a half hour later when they reached

61

the house. They had raced as fast as they could through the woods. Ralph held branches away to speed the journey for George without hindrance.

George lifted her gently into the backseat. Martha came running with a blanket. She stood with the arms reached out to the men then silently held her hands over her mouth.

"I'll drive her to the hospital. You and Ralph can follow directly behind me."

Chapter Eight
Third Victim's Treasures

Arriving at the cabin, he had developed a limp. It was near dawn. He would have to go to work without sleep. He cleaned up, ate eggs and bacon, put on the coffeepot, shaved, and then looked around the home for any traces of his recent baby doll. The sheets had blood on them. He grabbed them, rolled them up, grabbed her dress, and looked for anything else. Satisfied, he ran to the hole near the fence, where he really hadn't finished earlier. The shovel lay against the fence. He quickly buried the evidence along with parts of her dress.

Packing a sandwich, he filled his gray-green Thermos bottle with coffee that perked while he did his chores. He whizzed out the door. He threw them in the cab and took his chainsaw, gas, and axe, arranging them in the truck box. He would have to sharpen the saw when he arrived at the wooded spot where he left off the day before. A couple of chainsaw files were in the glove compartment in the cab. The Ford pickup clanked its way down the road shortly afterward.

* * * * *

Dr. Scott opened a door for Ralph Carter as he followed him with Anna Belle in his arms. George remained in the small waiting room.

"Lay her here, Ralph. You and your wife may stay if you wish," Dr. Scott said to Ralph at the hospital.

"I'll wait in the waiting room. Call me when you are ready to tell me what you have found. She deserves privacy and all that you can give her. I'll be praying for her and you too, Doc," George said.

Dr. Scott looked at his nurse, Judy. "I'll need you in here." She quickly followed.

"Pulse rate is one-hundred-thirty-eight, patient appears to be in a comatose state." He explored her body from her head, arms, and hands down to her feet.

Judy quickly documented the results on a chart for Anna Belle Carter.

"The girl appears to be around thirteen based on her development, but her father said she is only eleven. There's a small gash on her lower left lip, multiple scratches on her arms and hands, as well as six fingernails are ripped off at the tips. Her legs and feet have suffered from the elements in the woods, as well as exposure to the weather, rough terrain, and having one foot without a shoe has caused severe tears and open sores. The other foot has a huge broken blister on the heel, which has drawn blood. There are bruises on her entire body, which indicates struggle or roughly used. Her privates are ripped severely, which will need immediate attention. Note she will need stitches to close the area where she was ripped open beyond the normal area of the private parts." He stopped his examination and looked at his nurse. "Judy, you will need to clean her entire body gently and call me when you are finished. Meanwhile, I will go out to talk to her parents."

Frank and Martha followed Dr. Scott out to the waiting room.

"Frank, Martha, I will be honest and to the point. Will you two and George come into my office, please?"

They followed down the hall and seated themselves. All three were on the edge of their seat.

"Relax, I know you are anxious to hear what I have found. Anna Belle is in a comatose state, which can take a few days to six months to awaken. When you talk to her, say good things, and be aware she can hear everything you say. So be careful and gentle. Do not ask her anything about what happened to her. She will be the one who will awake to each part as she remembers. Her mind is healing from the shock she has endured.

"We are cleaning her now, I will tend to the wounds, and then we will take her to her room here in the hospital. She will get the very best treatment here, and you may visit her each day until she is released. We will keep close watch for her revival. This part is crucial, as she will need familiar voices and people to help her adjust back to normal. Let's hope she regains consciousness in a short while. The rest is in God's hands."

Anna Belle was placed comfortably in a room with lots of light and sun on the south corner of the hospital. Martha had never seen the hospital and was surprised to find it was located just off the main drive in a huge mansion, yellow in color with white trim. "What a beautiful home you are going to live in, Anna Belle," Martha said to the daughter who appeared to be oblivious to what she was hearing.

Dr. Scott had talked to the nurses so the staff was ready for the young girl. They picked the bedroom with a front window where the sun stayed for the better part of the day. She would need that. A cheery room with her mother sitting in a rocking chair next to her bed would be the very best visual she could possibly get to help her remember and become well again.

A small cot was placed in Anna Belle's room for Martha, as it was decided that she would stay with her. Ralph would bring extra clothing for Martha the next day. They would live from day to day until their little darling was back with them.

* * * * *

He returned home from the woods exhausted. Instead of eating, he fell on the bed with all his clothes on and was asleep immediately.

When he awoke, he could think clearer. He knew she couldn't be far. He had to find her, but he would look on the weekend, on a pretense of hunting squirrels. Perhaps she was already home. Maybe they, the authorities, were looking for her at this very moment. Or her parents. And what would they do to him? Give him the same treatment he had given to their daughter? That could be painful. He would never be the receiver. He needed to be the one in control. *But I'll have to be nice, until I know they are on to me.*

He paced around the cabin thinking, *I haven't seen anyone around here, no new automobile or truck tracks on my sandy road. I should get a newspaper, maybe my boss will give me his. I'll check out the obituaries from that sheriff's wife, Maria's, paper. Then I can rest at peace. I should have made sure she was dead before I left the cabin to dig her grave. Grave! I'll have to completely return it to ground level, camou-flage it, and restore it to its natural state.*

He took the shovel and scooped all the sand back, leveled it out. He placed his old tires over the bare sand. He had a pile of old fence post laying against the tool shed, so he put these on top of the tires. He took his hat off, scratched his bald head, and wore a satisfied grin. The deed was done.

He walked with a resolved strut back to the cabin of course his limp grabbed him in pain halfway back. He reached the door and entered, thinking he would have something to eat, when the late afternoon sun revealed Anna Belle's other shoe, which had fallen and rolled under his bed. It made him so mad, he knocked a dish off the counter where it smashed into several pieces. He stomped into the small bedroom, reached under the bed to retrieve the shoe, where he found her locket necklace as well. The chain was broken. He pried the little heart open. The picture was of her, with little golden curls framing her shy, dreamy-eyed face. He held it to his chest and knew he would have to keep this as a keepsake, a token for him to return to when he needed to remember how wonderful she had made him feel.

In his top dresser drawer, there was a small cigar box. In it was a scrap of Sarah's strawberry blond hair and a bracelet he had taken off Jenny's wrist after he bashed her head in with a rock. He remem-bered he had snipped a strand of hair off Sarah, his wife, just before he sprinkled lye over her head and face where she lay wrapped in a sheet in the grave. *Stupid, she was just stupid!*

However, I have my treasures, I should get a box at the hardware store with a lock on it, just in case. He shoved the cigar box back under his handkerchiefs and pushed the drawer shut. *That damn shoe. I'll just burn it with the trash.*

Chapter Nine
A Break from Duty

The last few strains of "Happy Birthday" could be heard at the Kaughman home.

"Happy Birthday, Susie. Are you ready to blow out the candles?" George asked his oldest child. Today she was eight years old; now was her time, her day. Her face beamed with excitement.

She looked from Mom to Dad and answered, "I'm ready. Little George, come and help me." Her younger brother grinned and climbed on her chair so he could reach the cake. Maria hoped he wouldn't spread his slobber all over it. Fortunately, Susie had the candles out before he gave a big wet puff.

Maria reminded Susie, "Remember, Susie, you must make a wish, think of something you really want, then take the first cut."

"Put your hand on mine. That's what I really want, your guidance for all my life, Mom."

Maria put her hand over Susie's and guided it until she had the first cut. George noticed a slight tear rest at the edge of Maria's eye. Pride filled his chest. *Who could ask for any more than this perfect family?* George silently thanked his creator for this wonderful bliss.

Chapter Ten
Search and Hide

He did finally get a paper from his boss, Frank Moreno, who hardly ever saw him. He worked independently but always got praise from his boss. Payday was their only contact, so it took at least two weeks before he was given the newspapers his boss had saved for him.

"Do you want me to keep saving them for you? I know you burn wood, so I will do that," his boss Frank asked.

"I'll take all of them. Giving them to me is a saving. Thank you, Frank." He smiled broadly.

Later after he was home, he searched the newspapers for one thing. The thing he was looking for was something about the little girl who got away. So far, there was nothing about her as far as an obituary. One of the first papers Frank Moreno had saved for him told a strange story of the discovery of a small child found in the woods, who was alive but it stated she was unknown. He felt some relief. However, who was she? Where was she now? He would have to be cautious and not say or make the wrong move.

* * * * *

Seven months had passed with no sign that Anna Belle would become conscious again. Early one morning, her mom, Martha, watched as Anna Belle slept. The sun filled the room with morning warmth. She thought she saw a motion. It appeared as if she saw Anna Belle's finger move. *Yes, it moved again.*

Martha rushed to her side and called out to her, "Anna Belle, are you awake?"

A small smile reached her face, and she opened her eyes, "Who are you? You sound like you know me, and you care for me." Anna Belle could hear the love in this strange woman's voice.

Martha hugged her child who was finally awake. "Honey, I'm your mother, you were in a coma, and I must go and call the nurse to come see the miracle. You are awake."

"Don't go yet. How long have I been in a coma?"

"I'll be right back, she's just out the door. You were in a coma over six months."

Anna Belle had a puzzled look on her face.

Martha told the nurse, Janet, that Anna Belle was awake. She quickly called Dr. Scott to let him know. Martha came back in the room with her. Nurse Janet had stayed with Anna Belle as much as her mother, Martha, had. Happiness beamed all over both women's faces. "How good it is to see you awake, Anna Belle. Are you hungry?"

"Yes, I am, but tell me more, how I got here?"

"Honey, we are hoping you can tell us what happened."

"I can't remember, Mother." She frowned. "I think I do recall you are my mom. But I can't remember why I am here. Where's my father?"

"He's home doing chores. I've been staying with you, but he will be coming today as soon as he hears you are awake."

Janet, the nurse, nodded to let Martha know she was calling Ralph. Just minutes passed when she returned with a smile. "Your dad is on his way now."

"Oh, goody, I will be so glad to see him. We can go home, right? I miss my dog and cats." She slid her feet and legs off the side of the bed. "Mom, help me, I want to get up."

Martha anticipated that she wouldn't remember anything. The doctors said Anna Belle would remember many things, but the traumatizing events would come slower, if at all.

"Honey, you will have to wait until Dr. Scott gets here and examines you before release. That shouldn't take long, but it will be his decision to let you return home." Her mom answered Anna Belle's question.

She reached for Anna Belle and hugged her close. "Be careful, sweetheart, that first step will be a hard one. You must be weak after being immobile for all those weeks." She weakly stood and took a couple of steps.

"Honey, your dogs and cats are all lined up and waiting for you right now."

"Silly Mom, they don't even know I'm coming."

"Let's get ready for Dad and Dr. Scott. They will be along soon, so we must be ready when they get here. We could pack up and have everything at the door. We can have breakfast too. By that time, they will be here. I miss your dad too. And home."

"You stayed here with me? Oh, Mom, you are the greatest."

"That's because I love you, sweetheart." Martha took a deep breath, hoping Anna Belle would be able to handle the shock of remembering. *How long will it take?* she asked herself. *Dear God, help her and keep her safe from that horrible evil man.*

Anna Belle sang while she packed all the things the hospital had given her, the many gifts from friends, as well as the clothes that hung in the closet in case she would need them before going home.

The doctor came in while they were packing. Anna Belle sat on the edge of her bed.

"Good morning, Dr. Scott, I'm awake."

"Well, look at the sleeping beauty. What prince kissed you on the cheek?"

"No one, I did it all by myself."

"Let's listen to your heart and take a pulse while I do it."

She sat obediently while he did his routine check. He listened through the stethoscope placing it here and there on her chest and back. "Everything is normal, Anna Belle, I'm thinking you can go home, but I want you to come in next week to see me, okay?"

"We're already packed. We knew you would release me, Dr. Scott. I'm going home. I'm so happy, all I want to do is dance."

"Knock. Knock." Anna Belle's father said from where he stood in the doorway to her room.

"Daddy, you're here!" She ran to him and hugged him for a long time. His face above her shoulder shined while tears filled his eyes. Once again, this day he thanked the Lord for this miracle after seven long months.

"I can't remember a finer day than this. How good it is to have you here, awake, and ready to take the journey home again."

Soon they were in the car and headed north to the Dixie Highway and to their farm.

Martha was sure the dark-headed man who hung in the entrance of the hospital was the one who had done what had happened to her daughter. She rode silently as her husband and Anna Belle talked endlessly about the farm and the dogs, cats, and the pigeons that lived in the hip-roofed barn cooing their sweet way of communication. Martha feared each moment, looking back to see if anyone was following them.

The long bumpy ride home was with very little event. No one followed or passed; in fact, there was no traffic this day going either way throughout the entire trip home. Martha silently laughed at her fears and thought about what they would do when they arrived home.

The gravel crunched under their wheels and soon the farm buildings fell into view. Anna Belle shouted out loud at the scene. "Mom, Dad, we're home at last! There's Panda, Rover, Dodger, Sweet Pea. They're all there just as I remembered them." The car was hardly stopped when she leaped out to greet her pets, laughing loudly.

Martha stayed back and touched her husband's arm, "Honey, we're going to have to take great care that the assailant isn't aware that she is home. She is in danger. He should never know she is alive. He will fear that she will tell who he is."

"I know, Martha, but we will eventually be seen and the news will come out. This is a job for George, and we must have faith in our Heavenly Father. Who knows, she may be the instrument that will enable George to catch him."

* * * * *

He had spent the last seven months wondering when he would see her again or if she was alive. Fear stabbed his heart. She could have wandered away and died somewhere, and no one would know what had happened to her. The newspaper never did tell the story about a girl missing. He was sure he hadn't missed any of the papers he had been given by his boss. But what if she was alive? He had to know.

He began to attend the church where George attended up on M-129, just north of town. He was careful not to talk to anyone, but he was all eyes and listened to the conversations. Just recently, he had heard that she was alive. He had no idea where she was, and the news didn't tell anything about her, so he waited and smiled at everyone. They all thought he was a very nice guy, maybe a little shy, because he didn't talk to anyone and only smiled and nodded. He scooted out of church before anyone else and drove home silently. George only knew that he lived across the road from where the bones of an unknown were found. He had not spoken to the man since that night. George thought he appeared to be a very congenial character, willing to talk about what he knew, but no more than that.

* * * * *

When no one was looking, he liked to check out the young girls who attended the church. So many to choose from. Soon he would be able to make a move on one of them. They were sweet little girls ripe for the picking, but stupid, and soon he would convince one of them to take a ride with him. Even that sheriff's daughter was getting to be a real beauty, looked just like her mother. She had George's blond hair and Maria's eyes were identical to their daughter, Susie's.

His working every day, cutting wood for his boss, kept him away from them. And now he was moving westward along the ridge, thinning out all the hardwoods. The drive was farther away, so much of his day was filled with travel and work. Yes, it was a good idea to attend church, so he could check out the next encounter and a tingling relief to his system. He needed that thrill, that feeling that surged in his entire body. Soon, it had to be soon.

Chapter Eleven
Jeffery Beacom

George was happy with the family. Each Sunday, they attended church. The children were growing like weeds. His wife was everything he needed to make his life worthwhile and a pleasure to go home to. But way back in his mind, the fact that that man was still on the loose gnawed at his conscience until he couldn't sleep. Had he moved? There were a few strange or unique men in the area that he had omitted as he researched their backgrounds.

Years had passed, and his days were spent confronting the trivial law breakers, speeding, fishing without a license, less and less trappers were around as the wildlife had thinned out. The market lacked a demand for the pelts, and once in a while, someone was beating their wife. The seriousness of the murders was another item. He needed a break in the case, before more bodies were found.

One day, Jeffery Beacom came into his office. He was his usual self, wearing the red suspenders and high boots with red striped socks above them. This day in particular, he was wearing a wide-brimmed straw hat. He chewed on a stalk of Timothy hay.

"Hello, there, George. Thought I'd come in and see how things are. What's new in the neighborhood?"

"What do you have on your mind, Jeffery?"

"Jest wonderin' if you have any leads on the murders."

"What murders?"

"Everyone knows about that girl out near Webb Road, and the bones found out there in the middle of nowhere with only one man living on the road. Kinda strange, isn't it?"

"I'm working on it, Jeffery. You have anything you want to tell me?"

"Not much. But I been thinkin' 'bout who and what for quite some time now."

"You're not alone, Jeffery. A day doesn't pass without my thinking about catching that rat who murdered the little girl off Webb Road, and I'm not sure the same one killed the one in that shallow grave." George looked into Jeffery's eyes. "And I'm getting closer as the days pass. I have a couple of people to talk to, and then I can draw some solid conclusions."

"Well, you let me know if you need me for anything, I'm right c'here ready to assist."

"Thanks, Jeffery, I'll remember that." George patted on Jeffery's back as they both walked out of the office and out into the sunshine. One went east while the other headed west on to their separate mission.

I've come a long way from investigating my best friend, Two Shoes's death till now. After a short period of time, I married Maria, who always was my right hand when it came to support. At thirty-eight, I was ready to have a family and enjoy my home life, away from the arrests and murders. Many asked me why I didn't go to fight for my country. That was an easy reply, keeping the law and order in my little town made me exempt. I have still to kick myself for not going in with Two Shoes. We could have fought side by side, but no, they would have separated us if they knew we were best friends. Frederick was exempt because of the farm, so both of us stayed home. I need to follow a lead, and I'll look up one of the suspects on my list. They're not really suspects but unusual, reclusive, quiet, leaving me and everyone else with very little to say about any one of the men on this list, but if I don't check, I may never find the murderer who is running loose.

George drove north out to the place where Chester Wilson lived. Most people called him Chet, and most thought of him as a quiet person who wasn't seen in town much. George was determined to talk to Chet and find out how quiet he was. Like where he came from, what he did for a living, and what he did in his spare time, all in a friendly conversation, so he wouldn't freeze up and not tell him what he wanted to hear. Of course, George knew he took care of the horses from Mackinaw Island in the winter, but he needed to know more than that.

Chet opened the door to his cabin when George stopped his car in front. "Hello, I thought I'd come out to visit with you. How's everything going?"

"What's on your mind, Sheriff, everything's going fine." He stood in the door wearing jeans, a plaid shirt with suspenders, and high-top leather boots. His hair was salt-and-pepper and needed a shampoo. His eyes and hair looked like his nap was interrupted.

"I've often wondered if you do much fishing."

"Fishing, are you kidding?" Chet grinned. "I don't take time to fish, summer or winter. Between feedin' the horses and cuttin' the wood for the fire, I'm tuckered out and just want to sleep."

"You mean, you don't have a hobby? I thought sure I saw you buying a checkerboard once in the hardware store."

"You're a strange one. You drive up here and ask me what I do with myself and if I have hobbies. What is this all about?"

"Oh, I forgot, I heard there was a horse running along the road and someone thought it was yours. Have any missing, Chet?"

He lifted his hand to his hair and scratched it. "Can't say as I have. Could have been anyone's, but I'll watch out for it. What color or markings did it have?"

"They said it was buckskin."

"Can you come in for a cup of coffee?" Chet stepped away so George could come in.

"Guess I will, Chet. You have some brewing?" This gave George a chance to check the inside for any clues and a look around. They had talked before, but Chet had not asked him inside his cabin.

It was dark and smoky inside, which took a few seconds to adjust to the lighting. George saw very little; a bed made of log was in the northeast corner, a fireplace was along the north wall, the familiar sink, pump for rain water, and basin to wash or shave. An old broken mirror hung above the basin. He had a small table with two chairs that didn't match and a davenport along the south wall where the sun could come in through the window in the afternoon. A couple of old rag rugs were spread on the wood floor.

Chet poured the coffee and asked George if he took anything in it.

"No, I take mine black."

"I like some sugar and a little cream. I get my milk from the farmer down a piece every other day, keeps it fresh. Like a cracker or something?"

"No, coffee's good enough. So are you game for a game of checkers?"

Chet grinned and said, "Sure."

He took the checkerboard box out from under the bed and quickly set it up.

They played three games, and during that time, George asked more questions. Most of the answers were vague or didn't relate to anything that would convince George one way or the other. This helped him by making a mental note to come back another time on the pretense of another set of checker games with Chet. By then, he might have found other leads that could convict or deny the suspicions about Chet.

George still had questions that needed to be answered before he checked him off the list. Was Chet the type who could tempt a child to get into his truck or car? Could he murder someone? What was his background? And finally, did he appear sane? If so, George planned to find the answers about Chet before he dismissed the idea that he could or would be the man he was looking for.

Chapter Twelve
The Woodsman's Past

The woodsman thought about his parents when he was driving home from working hard in the woods that afternoon after attending church the day before. He remembered how his father, Gus, told him that he was born in Greece in 1879. Gus came to America via a freighter where he accepted a job working in the boiler room stoking the fire with coal. It was a hot and dirty job, but it was taking him to the new world and freedom from a life of poverty. His grandparents had passed away after a long life growing potatoes, harvesting them and selling in the fall to pay for the land they lived on. His father had nowhere to go and hated potatoes since they ate them all three meals for as long as he could remember. He could remember how short his father was; he fit quite well down in the lower parts of the freighter where the ceilings were no more than six feet high, he had told his son. When they ported at Anchorage, Alaska, his dad went to shore and didn't return to the ship.

The truck hit a rut and jarred him back to reality. His thoughts went back to his father, the Greek. Gus was a short man with a dark complexion with blue eyes the color of the sky. He chuckled to himself remembering. Gus was looking for a job in Anchorage when he met a beautiful blond who worked in a saloon. She sold drinks, danced with the patrons, and other things. She stood tall with heels that made her tower over many of the men, her long blond hair piled high on her head with three curls hanging over her shoulder, her deep voice—*That comes with smoking and too much use of the voice*, he thought. However, Gus fell in love with her right away. He was indignant because he didn't think she should be working doing these things.

"That was your first wrong step, Gus, you should have never told her you wanted her for yourself. Look where it took you, Dad," he said out loud.

His thoughts went back to the story his father told him. Gus and Helen left Alaska and were married much later when she became pregnant. By this time, the couple was in Minnesota, working in the woods. They were just scraping the barrel to survive. Helen was pregnant, so she couldn't work any longer, at least until the baby was born in a couple of months, so Gus took on two jobs. He cut timber during the day and washed dishes in the local restaurant until they closed at ten o'clock. Helen became the general and snapped at him for many things that led him to disrespect his father because he cow towed to her every whim.

She did however work very hard. She took him to the woods, with his parents, almost right away after he was born. She breast fed him and loved him. Meanwhile, he lay bundled in a nest of sawdust. It was almost four decades later that they heard the timber in Upper Michigan was being milled and cleared with jobs galore. The pay was at a peak, and the family moved to the Cedarville area.

After Gus died, he had his mom, Helen, who nagged him the same as she did Gus. She sure wasn't that beauty his dad described to him in his story. He wouldn't take it, so he ignored her. Finally, she died of a heart attack. He missed her cooking, but that was about all. Just the same, he always showed love to her, and she never suspected his true feelings.

Chapter Thirteen
Hanna

He couldn't keep his thoughts off the little girl he caught sight of one Sunday at church. She was ripe for picking. He had to know more about her. He would wait for her and the family to leave for home after church, nodding to the people who waved at him. He always gave an obliging smile to all who spoke to him. Everyone thought he was a very special man. *Why would such a great and kind man be someone who would assault and murder little girls. He just wasn't the type*, he thought while he grinned secretly.

It was a few weeks later he had an opportunity to talk to Hanna. He told her she was a beautiful child.

"Oh, you are teasing me," Hanna said as she giggled.

He loved the giggle; it thrilled him. "I'm not teasing, I'm being very honest."

"Thank you, I've got to go." She ran out to her parents' car where her parents and brother waited for her.

He could hardly hold back his joy. He had finally spoken to her. He drove home smiling all the way. Soon, it won't be long now.

Three weeks had passed since he talked to Hanna. She smiled at him or waved as she drove away with her family. He bided his time until the right day arrived.

Soon after that, he met her in the hall between the sanctuary and the restrooms. He held out a flower to her. She reached out and took it, smiling. "Thank you." She blushed and carried it with her Bible in to find her family.

That was all he needed to feel the time was right when she could talk to him.

One sunny day, about a month later, he asked her to meet him on the Swede Road after school the next day. He wanted to show her something very exciting. He promised it wouldn't take long.

"Okay, I'll be there."
"Meet me around four?"
"Yes." She blushed and smiled. The look of love filled her eyes. *I've got her, the sucker. Tomorrow I'll get her.*

Chapter Fourteen
Maxwell Stuart

George went east of Cedarville toward DeTour Village to a boat dock and rented a boat to ride out to Little La Salle Island. Formally the island was called Bosley Island which is located due south of Cedarville nearly two miles away, through Bosley Channel to the dock on the southern tip where Maxwell Stuart lives. It was out a way, but the water was calm and the sun was shining. It was a good day to troll across Urie bay, and possibly get a fish or two, and look up Maxwell Stuart. He brought along his pole, a minnow bucket, and a short handled net. This trip would be pleasure mixed with work.

Maxwell lived in a mansion of a home high off the shore where his boat house was. George ascended steps that had been built of flat stone as they curved their way up and away from the dock. The gray walls and barn-red-trimmed home came into view through the pines and poplar trees as he approached, finding a man chopping wood. He could hear the ax hit the wood even before he saw him.

"Hello, there," George called out, so as not to startle him. "Are you Maxwell Stuart?"

"Yes, I am." Maxwell noticed that George wore a pair of jeans, a plaid shirt with the sleeves rolled up, and a straw hat. However, he did recognize he was the sheriff.

"I have been fishing and realized I forgot to bring water. I wonder if you would give me a drink."

"Sure, I have a dipper here on the well pump, make yourself to home."

"Do you have a quart jar for me to take? I plan to fish all day," George asked, knowing this may allow him to check out his home and surroundings, if he could work a conversation up.

"I think I can find one here in the basement, follow me." He motioned to George.

The basement door was just a few feet away from the pump. The creaking of the little used basement door surprised George. Mentally he thought it strange he didn't oil it or possibly didn't use it at all.

Maxwell reached for a flashlight on the shelf to the right of the door and turned it on so they could see as they entered. There were rows of jars, some full as well as empty ones on a different shelf. George was surprised to see a clean neat dirt floor storage area, where the canned fruit and vegetables were stored.

"Here, this one will work." Maxwell handed it to George, turned off the flashlight, and replaced it to the same spot where he found it.

"Maxwell, do you live here alone?"

"Most of the time, yes, Sheriff, I do. My family does come from time to time, but they are from Detroit and Ferndale, so it would be only a week vacation or a long weekend. My daughter lives in Detroit, where she teaches school, and my son is in Ferndale, where he took over the business. I have my peace and quiet here enjoying the wild life and birds."

"Do you get to the mainland very often?"

"Sure, I have a motorboat with a small cabin, a wooden Chris Craft, which works grand when I don't plan to come home right away."

"Oh, you stay on the boat while you're visiting on shore?"

"Yes, it works quite well and is comfortable. Rocks me to sleep after a couple drinks."

They both laughed. He reached for the pump, rinsed out the canning jar, and filled it with fresh water. George got serious. "What about your private life, do you have a girlfriend or wife?"

"Not at the present. Why?"

"Just wondered, a man could get lonesome out here all alone."

"Hey, come out with it, what's on your mind, Sheriff?"

"I'm looking for someone who has spent a lot of time here and doesn't have a girlfriend or wife to satisfy his needs. I may be way off, but I'm looking for a man who looks elsewhere for what comes naturally. To be quite blunt, I'm looking for someone who likes young girls."

"Are you accusing me, a man of stature? I am a man who is reputable with a huge amount of clout, money, and friends. How dare you?"

George smiled and answered, "Just doing my job, Maxwell. Sorry if I ruffled your feathers."

"You sure did, and I don't take it lightly."

"Understandable, but if you're innocent, it shouldn't bother you."

"I am innocent of doing anything against anything such as assault and murder."

"I didn't ask you if you assaulted or murdered anyone, and you know it, I asked you if you had a lady friend for companionship. Then it turned into this sorry conversation. Do you want to go with me to the county sheriff's office to talk to the sheriff there?"

"Why would I need to go with you? I'm not your man."

"You have nothing to worry about if you can prove that, Maxwell. Thanks for the drink of water. I'll be on my way. I'm sure we'll talk again when the time is right."

Chapter Fifteen
Foul Play with Mixed Emotions

Hanna waited on Swede Road. She became tired and began walking back toward M-129. She really wanted to see him, but he was late, and she would be missed. Secretly she thought she was in love with him. Her heart jumped when she saw him, just as it did when she saw him approaching with his old pickup. His smile lit her entire face up. She liked his dark curly hair too. It curled up around the band of his hat. This made him more handsome than anyone she knew.

She had been sitting down in the grass at the edge of the road, so it surprised him when he saw her. He stopped the truck and rolled down the window. "Hello, little baby doll, have you been waiting long?"

"Not really." She opened the truck door, and he reached to help her in. "What are you going to show me, sir?"

"Why, baby doll, I'll tell you when we get there." He drove east along the dusty road toward the quarry. They passed a couple of farms and finally reached the limestone piles all along either side of the road. The workers had gone for the day, so he drove back where they were mining. He stopped the truck. "I wanted you to see this." He gestured with his hand pointing to the many piles of limestone and the mining equipment. She looked all around the massive pit. He told her, "This is where the workers dynamite the limestone and separate the dolomite out for one of the three conglomerates to make steel." He looked at her as she observed the massive pit with her mouth open in surprise.

"And this is what I want to show you too." He grabbed her and kissed her. She pulled away. He laughed and grabbed her again.

"Don't, I don't want you to do that."

"Sorry, baby doll, I'm going to anyway, even if you don't want me to."

He reached and locked the door so she couldn't get out. "Touch this."

"No."

He grabbed her and forced her against her will. She screamed, so he held his hand across her face. She kicked and writhed underneath his weight. He continued until she bit him in the hand. With that, he hit her. She screamed some more, so he hit her again and again until she quit fighting. His body arched and fell against her.

A few minutes passed when he finally realized he would have to bury her in the limestone pile. He took his shovel and dug a shallow grave alongside and parallel with the truck. He dragged her limp body out of the truck, her head hitting the edge of the seat and rocker panel, then along the gravel and into the gravesite.

Within minutes, he threw the shovel in the back and headed west back to home. This time he didn't find anything he wanted for a keepsake, he was satisfied, he loved hearing her scream, as she struggled and fought him. It was enough for now; he would hold on to the memory, the thrill of the experience. He took all the back roads and trails where there were some from hunters. Luckily, no one passed him from either direction, until he was well on his way home and safe.

* * * * *

Meanwhile, Hanna's parents wondered where she was. She didn't get off the school bus at the regular time. Her mom, Rose, called the school, but they had all left for the day. She called the principal, Thomas Greenly, at his home. His wife answered and said he hadn't returned from school yet but would tell him as soon as he returned.

Mrs. Greenly wondered if her husband, the principal, took her and would bring her home after he had bought the groceries. But why would he have taken her, unless he promised her a prize for being the all A student this week? Mrs. Greenly remembered her husband telling her that Hanna was the honor student this week.

Another hour passed, Rose ran to meet her husband Pete. "Hanna didn't come home from school, Pete. I'm so worried, where can she be?"

"Have you called her friend Carol? She may have gone there after school."

"She wouldn't do that unless she had asked first." She reached for the phone as she talked. "Hello, is Hanna there with your daughter?"

"Why, no, she isn't. Have you called the school office?"

"I tried, but they're all gone for the day. I was able to reach Mrs. Greenly, but her husband isn't home yet."

"I'm sorry, Rose, but if I do see Hanna, I'll call right away."

Rose called the sheriff next. "Sheriff George, my daughter Hanna didn't come home from school today. She isn't at her best friend Carol Dale's home either. I'm so worried, I need your help to find her."

George's stomach churned making it ache. *Not another missing girl*, he thought.

"I'll get right on it and don't worry until I check a few places where she may be. First of all, relax, and know that your husband Pete is with you for comforting and pray to your Heavenly Father that she is found. Have faith and know that he is there."

George felt immediately that there was foul play. This had happened three times in the past three to four years. First, it was Jenny Adams, out west of town in a ditch across the old Miller farm; second, it was the buried bones found of another young woman or child, could be done by the same man; then Anna Belle, who did survive but still had amnesia and was in jeopardy until the man was found. And now Hanna was missing.

This kind of horrific event has never happened in the history of his experience as sheriff for near to twenty years. It was too coincidental to be isolated deaths. He was sure the culprit was a serial killer. He believed he was a serial killer; he knew he was a sociopath and possibly a psychopath. But so far, no one in the area appeared to be this kind of character. This person was thoroughly evil. George needed to find out where Hanna was as soon as possible. He prayed he would find her before it was too late.

He went home. Maria was in the kitchen cooking. "Where are Susie and Little George?"

"In their bedrooms. Susie's doing homework, and George is pestering her to play monopoly with him. Why? You look upset, George, is everything all right?"

"Another young girl is missing. You know Hanna Franklin? She didn't come home on the bus today. Her mom, Rose, called me to let me know. She was so upset, I tried to calm her down and reminded her to pray and relax. I can't think where to look first. Maria, would you check with the family and see if they will be willing to have you put something in the paper to help. I called the Mackinaw Sheriff Department in St. Ignace to alert them. They will be on the lookout as well as checking the border."

"First of all, George, let's pray for the family and Hanna's safety. Only God knows where she really is. But we need to ask for guidance, peace, and understanding, how and why we are confronted with another missing child."

They held hands and called upon the Lord for help. They said they understood it is his will and not ours in all things. They asked for comfort for the Franklin family. When George finished, he held Maria close and said, "I hope I never have to experience anything near what the Franklins are at this moment."

Maria kissed him and said, "God will look after us and our Susie and young George. He always has."

The next day, no news came in about the missing girl. Soon a week passed without news. What George feared gnawed at his mind, until he had to take action, checking out the two who he had talked to before and plan to see the third man he wondered about.

The missing girl was fresh, and he could ask what they did yesterday and pinpoint the time element at precisely around 3:30 to 4:00 p.m. and later that evening.

He drove north up to see Chet Wilson. When he arrived there, he could see his pickup wasn't in the yard. He knocked at the cabin door. Just a hollow noise reached him, no footsteps were heard or door opening. He walked out to the back where Chet chopped his wood and stacked it in a lean too, but he wasn't there either. As he walked back to his car. He looked for fresh footprints and tire tracks in the grass and gravel yard out to the driveway where his car sat. It appeared they were older, and Chet had not been home last night at all.

George took out his notebook and put the time and what he observed down on a page with the days date. He decided to go out to Little LaSalle Island to see Maxwell Stuart. The drive was pleasant in spite of his not being able to talk to Chet. Some fog would appear as he drove nearer to the water, while the road curved in and out along the shore. Soon the morning sun would burn off the fog with a promise of another beautiful day. A half hour later, he was launched in a small motor boat he rented from the local boat dock. He headed due south to the island.

It only took fifteen minutes to reach the beach where Maxwell docked his boat in a boat house. George reached over and tied the rope to one of the pier logs. Then stepped out on the dock and began the ascent to Maxwell's home.

The bees were humming and buzzing around Max's flower beds. George heard a door open. "Saw you coming from the dock on land. I just finished breakfast, do you want some coffee?"

George reached out the canning jar he had borrowed from him and shook his hand saying, "Yes, I'll take a cup, nothing in it, I take it straight."

"What brings you back here today, George?"

He sipped his coffee and looked straight into Max's eyes. "I have to talk to you about where you were yesterday afternoon, Max. There's been an incident."

"What incident? I was here all day and never went anywhere, George."

"You never left the island for even an hour to get supplies?"

"I suppose someone saw me, is that it?"

"So you were on land for a while yesterday, where did you go, and what did you do while you were there?"

"Yes, I was there. I was seeing a young lady who seems to care for me a lot. And that's all I'm going to say. It's private."

"I respect your private life, Max, but—"

Whack!

All 240 pounds and six-foot-three body of George, the sheriff, hit the floor with a thud.

"What did you do that for?"

She looked at him, dumbfounded, and answered, "I thought you'd want to get him out of our business."

When George woke up, he was in his car at the pier on the mainland.

* * * * *

The sun warmed the evil one's face waking him the next morning. It made him realize he had overslept; his boss had mentioned that he would be out to the stand of timber to give him his paycheck early as he was going down state for a few days.

His thoughts languished in the thrill of yesterday. So she died, they all did one time or another. It was evident that he couldn't let her live. After all, she knew who he was, and she would squeal like a pig the second she saw her parents. Yes, she had to die.

No one would find her for a long time. He picked the right spot and pile of limestone. The company workers would have to remove the many piles ahead of that one near the far back of the property. No one would suspect him even if he was seen picking her up. Everyone knew him as being a nice guy who works hard in the timber business. A man only goes to town once a month for supplies and once a week to church. He prayed when he was asked to, and he was just the greatest person ever.

He got dressed quickly, grabbed a couple of sandwiches made of peanut butter and jelly that his mother had canned. Even though the canned goods were four years old, the jelly was still good. He took a shortcut toward the location near the far end of the ridge of hard wood.

As he drove past the Carter Farm, on his shortcut, he noticed that Ralph and Martha was talking to a young girl, "No, it can't be Anna Belle, she's in St. Ignace at the hospital," he said out loud. But it was Anna Belle.

I need to do something about this, he thought. *If she recognizes me, it will be the end for me.*

He drove just a little faster, trying to get by before they looked up as all farmers do, since they don't see traffic that often. He hoped the dust from the sandy road would conceal the identity of his truck. The last ten miles brought him up to the spot where he had quit the afternoon before. His boss was waiting for him.

"Hey, you are late. First time I can remember in a long time," his boss said.

"I slept like a baby last night and woke with a start, realizing it was late, boss."

"Well, here's your check. I'll be getting on. I'll stop back at the cabin. I already packed, and I'm ready to enjoy a long weekend down state. I'll stop over at your house when I get back."

"Thanks, Frank, I promise I will be on time and get this area cleared before you return. The best way to catch me is here in the woods. I usually go home, eat, and go to bed. I'm so tired."

"You are a very hard worker, I can't deny that, so I'll see you when I catch you."

Frank smiled at him and nodded his head, lifted his hat, and turned toward his truck. He stuffed his check in his pocket, checked the chainsaw, filled the gas tank, oiled the areas that needed it, and began to sharpen the chain. He smiled to himself contentedly. He even had his boss buffaloed.

His smile faded when he remembered who he saw on the way to work. "That pig got away. Well, I'll fix her as soon as the right opportunity arrives," he said to himself. "Yes, she will be sorry for running away and cheating me of another round with her before I buried her. She'll be sorry for not dying. It's just a matter of time for her."

Chapter Sixteen
A New Experience

Work absorbed most of the woodsman's time. His hard work deterred him from doing his evil deeds like the one he had done just a few days prior. He dived into his work with gusto, after the time spent with Hanna. He regretted her not liking his roughness. He could have enjoyed her a few more times.

Weeks passed and his work took him west along the vast ridge from the Cedarville area toward Rudyard. He felled many trees each day. His skidder helped him mechanically stack the logs for shipping out of the woods. He didn't waste any of the timber. The branches were cut into shorter lengths for firewood. The smaller twigs were stacked and cut finely with the chainsaw, so they eventually would rot into the soil. The day was long and tiresome. He cut twenty trees down, trimmed off the branches, and stacked the fire wood. He returned to the trunks and cut them into lengths of eight to ten feet depending on the length of the tree trunk. He stopped the chainsaw to refuel it. After he was finished, he began to stack the small branches in a pile to clear all the debris and have a clear road to drag out the logs. Soon it was time to head home. The day's work was over, the sun would fall behind the woods, and it would become dark here before it would at home where there was a clearing in his area.

He headed east to the Pea Line Road then north. He saw a little girl sitting on the porch crying. She was all alone, so he stopped to see if he could help her. "Hello, what's the problem? I saw you were crying. Is there anything I can do to help you?"

"My mom and dad aren't home and the door is locked. I can't get in."

"Do you want me to stay here until they get home?"

"Would you? I'm afraid to be here alone."

"What's your name, baby doll?"

"My name is Marjory."

"That's a beautiful name, goes with you quite well. You are a real beauty."

She laughed and said, "Thank you, you are kind to stay with me."

Yes, he thought, *I will stay. I can use some more refreshments.*

"Do you want to see my baby pig?"

"Sure, is it in the barn or in that shed to the right?"

"It's in the small shed to the right. My baby pig has nine sisters and brothers." She opened the shed door to squealing and grunting noises. The sow lay on her side in a position to feed her brood. They were fighting to get the best teat to suckle on.

The stench was more than he could stand. He held his breath and thought of the reward he would get if he remained and told her how cute the little baby pig was.

"He is so cute. Do you have a name for him?"

"Yes, he is Elmer, and I'm going to name the rest as soon as Daddy says I can." There was a heat light hanging over the pen so the little ones would keep warm. The mother stayed away from the heat and lay along the fence.

"Let's go out and see if your parents are coming yet, Marjory."

"Okay, I love to watch them, but we can go up to the house now if you want to."

As they walked up the lane to the house, he touched her ringlets and asked, "Where did you get those beautiful long black curls, Marjory?"

"My mom has black hair too. She cuts hers off because she thinks it's too hard to keep the tangles out of mine and hers too."

"Want to go for a ride?" he asked her. "I forgot to get something from the spot where I was working."

Her eyes lit up and looked excited. "I sure do! It won't take too long, will it?"

"No, it won't take too long, we'll be right back."

"Good, 'cause if my parents get back, then they will worry too."

"Don't worry, we'll be back."

He helped her into the truck and headed back south and west to the timber area where he had piled the wood that day. He walked with her to an area where the deer had packed the tall grass down.

"You can sit here where it is soft and comfortable. I'm going to get the tools I forgot."

It was all he could do to keep his hand off her, but it had to be just right. She seemed to be content to sit there, so he walked away on the pretense of getting a tool he had hid with the others. While he was gone, he took off his outer overalls and his quilted shirt, then came back, and told her to lie down on the shirt so it would be comfortable.

"Why do you want me to lie down?"

"So you can relax. It's been a long day for you, hasn't it?"

"Yes, but…"

He reached for her. "My baby doll, you are so beautiful." He began kissing her then held her down. She tried to get away, but he was taller, stronger, and determined to have her.

She struggled, and he laughed in delight. "No one can hear you, so it's no use to yell, baby doll."

He continued, "We're out in these woods miles away from anyone near, so be a good girl and let me try to relax with you."

It took a long time to tug and pull all the smaller branches he had trimmed off the twenty trees he cut that day back over her. He piled them high and thick. He walked all around the pile to make sure no one could see her body. He would burn the brush pile before she began to rot and send out a foul odor. Every piece of evidence would be in ashes left to fertilize the ground.

With one exception, he would have a lock of her long black ringlets. He patted his pocket and smiled with a satisfied expression.

Chapter Seventeen
A Helper

George got out of his car and went back to the pier with plans to return to Little LaSalle Island. He started the boat motor and headed across the bay. Once he was there, he cautiously took out his gun, took off the safety, and held it ready. Each step was guided as he crept closer and closer to the mansion. Instead of using the steps, he went along the tree line and came out near the backdoor. There were no lights on in the house. He tried the door to see if it was locked. It opened. The silence was deafening; all that could be heard was the refrigerator running and the crickets chirping outside.

As he advanced across the kitchen, he slowly looked each way in case Max was hiding in readiness to leap out at him. The bathroom was clear, he knew he needed to go upstairs, so he carefully inched his way one step at a time, making sure he stepped to the side so the loose boards wouldn't squeak. On the landing, he could see four doors. Two were open, so he looked in each one first. No one was there either. He had looked in the closets as well. Next he went to the door at the end of the hall. It was the master bedroom, which took the larger part of the upstairs. The door opened noiselessly, revealing a large poster bed, a couch, chairs, and a private bath room adjoining the bedroom. He realized Max wasn't there either.

There is just one more room remaining, George thought as he went back into the hall and walked sideways along one wall, the one without pictures hanging, until he reached the last room with the door shut. He slowly turned the knob and cracked the door open then waited to see if he could hear anything from within the room. He heard a slight scratchy noise of a branch tapping on the window from the wind outdoors. He bravely pushed the door open and walked in. It was empty. He walked back to the stairs and rushed out of the house. It was obvious Max was gone.

George took the steps two at a time down to the pier, jerked the rope to start the boat engine, and headed north back to the mainland. He tied the boat to the dock and walked to the office to pay Herb Mash for the boat rent.

"Hi, Herb, how much do I owe you for the use of the boat?"

"You don't owe me anything, George. I know you are busy looking for that Hanna girl, and I just can't charge you after all the things you do for the people of Les Cheneaux area."

"Maybe you can tell me if you saw Max today or last night come over with a girl. They may have taken the boat beyond here, but I'm wondering if you did see anything?"

"I did see him with a young woman, she looked about twenty-one or twenty-two years old. They seemed like they were in love. They couldn't stop smiling at each other."

"You don't say?"

"Could the twenty-one-year-old be younger wearing lots of makeup on to make her look older?"

"It's possible, I wasn't that close."

"When did you see them?"

"I saw them last night before you left."

"Thanks, Herb, for your help and the boat."

Herb just grinned and crossed his arms. "It was nothing. Anytime, George."

George headed to the car, asking himself, "Was it Hanna with Max, that abducting dog, he hit me in the head and ran off with her." He touched the spot where he was hit and winced at the pain that shot through his head. How could he do this while living on his private island? Did he have a cabin on the main land where he could stay part-time?

George pulled into the office where he saw Jeffery Beacom sauntering down the street. Jeffery picked up speed when he saw George arrive on the scene. "Hey, George, what's new?"

"That's my question, Jeffery. You seem to know more than I do when it comes to the latest gossip or truth. Come on in the office, I need to talk to you."

Jeffery swung in to the office right behind George and took a seat across him. Old Abe Lincoln looked down at him as he thought, *Honest Abe. I'd better keep it straight whatever George asks me.*

"I have a couple of people I'm wondering about. I think you can tell me something about each one, but I want you to swear to secrecy on an oath before I touch on the subjects. Do you want some coffee?"

"Yes, coffee sounds good, and I swear. Do you have a Bible?"

George reached in his top drawer and pulled out a King James Version of the Holy Bible. Jeffery quickly jumped over the desk to touch the cover of the Bible and said, "I swear to secrecy all of the things we talk about today, so help me, God."

Smiling inside, George handed Jeffery a fresh cup of coffee his wife had just brewed and sat across from Jeffery. "I'll start with a man who lives on Little LaSalle Island."

"Maxwell Stuart, he's retired and near a millionaire. He lives on the island alone. He owns the entire island. He likes younger women. And he is with a different one every time I see him."

"Can you tell me anything else? For instance, do you know if he has a home or cabin here on the mainland?"

"I dunno, but I'll find out."

George handed him a new notebook. "Here, write it down." He handed him a pencil also.

"There's another man I'm wondering about. He comes to church on Sunday morning, short like you, speaks French, smiles a lot."

"That's Andre Toulouse. He moved here from Canada, around twelve years ago. He is a quiet one, he is. He is a hermit, keeps away from the rest of us, never takes time for any community affairs, and lives in the woods north east of here, over on Swede Road, off and back, way back in the woods in a log cabin. I can hear him play the piccolo in the evening from my place. That's what they say, it's him playin'."

"He doesn't work?"

"Can't say as I know what Andre does."

"Write it down. Find out."

Jeffery added a number two with a period behind and wrote, "Andre, work?"

"Is there anything else, George?"

"Do you know Garde Kangas? I have been told he lives in his grandfather's home. His father was a woodsman who died in an accident. A tree fell on him while his father and he were cutting for fire wood. Does this refresh your memory?"

Jeffery stood up and walked around the room thinking. Then he settled back in his chair and answered, "The guy's a little touched. He lives on a disability check. He just has a garden and cans the vegetables or stores the potatoes in a cool place to keep them through the winter and into the next season. You know people talk, and that's all I know from what others say. He did work as a hired man at the Wilson farm a couple times off and on when they need an extra hand to do the harvest."

"Do you know if he has a temper?"

"I never saw him if he does."

"Write that down too, and see what you can find out about his nature, like a temper, if he acts shady or something out of the ordinary. When you find out, let me know. That's when I'll look him up and have a word with the three." George didn't tell Jeffery he had already talked to Maxwell, or Chet, he would have to keep this to himself until he had more to go on. For now it would be on hold until he found Hanna and Maxwell.

Jeffery stood up and saluted George and said, "See you around, George. I have a job to do."

George shook his hand and smiled. He knew it would be hard for Jeffery to keep his sworn vow, but he knew he would try to. He remembered at the same moment that he could remember Andre Toulouse did come to church in a clean shirt and jeans, both of which were worn with age. In spite of his appearance, he hid a secret about where he worked, still he always placed an offering in the collection plate on Sunday regularly.

George went out to the Wilson farm to find out what they knew about Garde Kangas. George found Bob Wilson out in the barn unloading hay.

"Hi, Bob, it looks like you're keeping busy. Do you need a hand?"

"Not this time. But I have hired a man from time to time."

"Is his name Garde?"

"Matter of fact, yes, it is his name." He looked up at George and asked, "Why?"

"Has he ever displayed a temper in front of you?"

"Only once did he get upset. He couldn't find a hammer he was using and became very unnerved." He shook his head slightly and added, "Later he explained he worried I would blame him for losing it, and he would have to buy me a new hammer."

"Bob, does he live alone?"

"Yes, he does."

"I'm going out to talk with Garde to find out more about him."

"You won't find him today, George. He's gone to Mackinaw Island for the day and will return back late tonight or early tomorrow morning. He did promise to come to work tomorrow, so you can reach him after that."

"Okay, thank you for your help, Bob." George turned toward his patrol car, waving as he left.

Chapter Eighteen
Excellent Clue

"Remember, George, Susie will be celebrating her birthday this week. Let me know if you can be home Friday evening for the family gathering," Maria reminded her husband.

"Honey, I'll try very hard. If there's nothing like an emergency, I promise I'll be here. I love you, sweetheart. Right now, I'll be in the office to catch up on my documenting the latest evidence toward catching that evil serial killer."

The phone rang as George entered his office. The man on the other end said, "I need to report my daughter missing."

"Wait, who is this?" George grabbed a notebook and a pen.

"It's John Sharp, over on the Pea Line, west of Pickford. We had an emergency and had to leave quickly over a week ago. We left a note on the door for our thirteen-year-old to go to the neighbors, but when we returned today, they told us she never went over there."

"Has anyone seen her? Has she been going to school? Have you asked around or called the school?"

"Yes, yes, I have tried everywhere, and no one has seen her. We are frantic with worry. You have to do something. We need your help. Dear God, hurry."

George's stomach churned into a knot. *Not another missing girl,* he thought.

"I'll be right out." He grabbed his hat, a notebook, and belted his pistol on. Maria was in the office with Susie and young George. "Honey, I'll be a while, going out on the Pea Line. There's another missing girl."

Maria put both hands to her mouth. "Oh, no, not again. Oh, George, those poor parents. It's so hard on them. Honey, I'll stay up until you return." She threw him a kiss.

His heart lifted for a second; she was the sunshine if his life, her and the children. His life would not be much without them. He looked forward to the birthday party that coming Friday night. He would be able to see his parents, his brother, and at least a couple of Susie's friends.

He drove north to the town line road at Pickford, then west out to the Pea Line.

He could see the lights shining in the window of the farmhouse as he approached.

"Hello," Mr. Sharp answered the door to George's knock. "Come in." Once in the door, he continued, "Have a seat. Honey, Sheriff George is here." John was standing on crutches with a leg cast and bandaged to above his knee.

She came out of the bedroom with red eyes and more tears on her face. "I can't stop crying, I blame myself, but we had to go so fast that we weren't thinking. Marjory is thirteen but immature. She didn't think to go to the neighbors. Our note blew off the door. John found it in the field where the wind blew it."

"Do you still have it?"

"No, I threw it in the trash."

"I will possibly need it for evidence. Would you please get it out of the trash?" George asked her patiently.

"Let's start at the beginning. What day was the emergency? Also please tell me what the emergency was."

George began to write. "On..." He looked up for the answer.

"It was ten days ago. John was out picking corn and caught his leg in the gears. It cut his leg up pretty bad, he was bleeding hard, and I had to take him to the hospital. I wrapped it up tightly and away we went toward St. Ignace. They took him to Petoskey by ambulance for surgery. There was no way to get to the neighbors. We tried to call several times without success. We assumed Marjory was with them, and we weren't worried, not until we came home and found she wasn't there with the neighbors. Now we are frightened to death, wondering where she is." She began hysterically crying again.

"Okay, so ten days ago," he wrote what she had said up to her last sentence. He also wrote that the school was contacted as well as any of her school friends. Betty continued crying, sobbing, and howling. John looked on with confusion and pain to see his wife taking things so badly.

"I can't promise you anything. She may show up, and if she does, please call me immediately. In the meanwhile, I'll be asking questions to dig up any clues about where she is and if anyone saw anything leading to where she can be. When you say neighbors, are you referring to the farm just north of the road to Rudyard?"

"Yes," Sharp said. "That's McDowell's." Betty broke down and began crying again.

George looked at her in sympathy knowing how she felt. He couldn't think what to say to make her fears go away.

"Okay, I'll stop there now on my way back. John, Betty, I'm hoping we can find out where she, Marjory, is."

"What are you going to the neighbors for?" John Sharp asked.

"Ask them if they may have seen anything unusual in the last few days."

"Oh, I see." The couple seemed to be in a daze.

George looked back at John Sharp standing with a crutch and bandaged leg. Betty quietly stood beside her husband with a sad forlorn look as they watched George leave.

George felt bad for them, just as he had for the parents of all the other girls that were missing. He prayed Marjory was with her girlfriend or some simple explanation for where she went.

There had to be a break, some clue that would unravel the whole case and lead to an arrest. With all the suspects, there had to be one who would make a mistake and lead him to the real killer. He left silently and drove north to the McDowell farm.

They had completed milking their dairy cows and had a late supper. Mrs. McDowell sat rocking in her chair knitting a pair of socks, while her husband sat beside her on the porch having a smoke.

George drove up the drive, with three collie dogs barking loudly and wagging their tails at the same time.

McDowell yelled at them and smiled at George as he got out of the sheriff car.

"What can I do for you, Sheriff?"

"I guess you know about Marjory Sharp missing?"

"Yes, John and Betty are pretty upset, for a good reason. It's a bad thing to happen to them. We're sorry Marjory never got the note they left for her."

George had his hat in his hand and looked away from it to the couple. "I'm here to ask a few questions. I'm wondering if you did see anything unusual happen in the last ten days. We believe that's when she came up missing, ten days ago. The Sharps had left a note for her saying she should come to your place if they weren't back. Betty locked the door, so she couldn't get in for shelter, so I believe she went somewhere that very day."

"Ten days, good grief." He shook his head. "Ma, what do you think?" He looked at is wife.

"The sheriff here wonders if we saw anything unusual in the last ten days concerning the missing girl, Marjory Sharp. Let's get our heads together and think." He spoke loudly as Mrs. McDowell was hard of hearing.

"Nothing, we are very busy with our chores and work here, I will say that there is very little traffic down that road, with the exception of two pickups that go by. One goes every day, but I don't know where it goes. The other goes about once a week or twice. And we never have seen whether it comes back out this way or keeps going."

"Yeah, that's right, one is a Ford, beat up some. The other is newer, a Dodge."

"Do you know what year either one is? Or what color it is?"

"The Ford is two-tone green. The Dodge is dark green, probably only one or two years old. It looks like new. That Ford looks like it is an early fifties model."

George wrote all the information down. This was the best lead he had in a long time. If he could get anything near the same from another witness, he could break the case.

Chapter Nineteen
Accident at the Fire

He was in the timbered off region burning the brush pile that covered the dead body of Marjory. The flames reached high in the air. The billowing dark smoke could be seen for quite a distance. He had used oil and gasoline to start the green brush burning.

His boss, Frank, saw it from his camp where he stayed during the week. The smoke was coming from the direction where his hired man was cutting. He jumped into his truck and headed over as fast as he could, in case the fire got out of control.

As Frank drove up, he saw the grass burning all around the pile and spreading. His hired man was beating it out with his coat. The flames were reaching higher. Frank jumped on his new skidder and moved it to safety. Next he grabbed a shovel and a rake. He had a barrel of water in the truck bed with a hose on it. With the two men working hard, they had the fire under control within a few minutes. Both men were exhausted from the struggle and adrenaline flow.

Frank took out a handkerchief and wiped the sweat from his brow. A look of relief was on his face, even though he was slightly miffed with his hired hand.

"Thanks, Frank, for coming along. It was getting away from me."

"I'll say. You should have known better. Why are you burning the brush pile? This is the first time you have done this."

"Well, you did say you wanted the area cleared, so I thought it would be good to have it gone." He knew he was lying, but it was all he could think to tell his boss.

Frank shook his head but smiled.

"You know, Frank, I wanted to ask you," he tried to change the subject, "I looked at the signature on my check, and I see it is Francisco Moreno. You don't look Spanish with your blond hair and height."

"I was adopted by my parents. They raised me and did a pretty good job. Sent me to college, but I quit. I disappointed them but..." Frank grabbed his head.

"Frank, what is it?"

"Help me. My head. Something's wrong."

He put him in the truck and headed toward St. Ignace hospital. The trip from that part of the woods took him past the farm where Marjory lived. He headed west to get to the road that went south to St. Ignace. He pulled up to the hospital forty-five minutes later. Frank's face had pulled down on one side, and he was lisping. The nurses brought him quickly in to the emergency room where the doctor on duty did all the things it would take to save his life.

A week later, he was admitted to an assisted living facility in an old three-story hotel in Cedarville. An ambulance drove up to the front door, where he was helped into a wheelchair and wheeled into his new home.

George was there along with Maria. They had heard about a man who had a stroke and lived through it. Maria wanted to get an interview for the paper. George was thinking she needed his support. He also was curious about this man because he was one of those he had on his list. He filled the description of a recluse, a person who keeps to self, and has a quiet personality.

Frank appeared in good spirits, even though he couldn't walk or use his left hand. He gave them a crooked smile and asked them to come in as soon as the nurses had him settled in.

Maria and George took a seat in the parlor, where there was an upright Wurlitzer piano, a long davenport, a couple of overstuffed chairs, and a fireplace where they could hear the cracking of the wood as it burned.

A nurse came for them about fifteen minutes later.

Frank greeted them. "Come on in, have a seat," he said with a lisp.

His room was cozy, with a standard bed, a couple of chairs, a small kitchenette, and a private bathroom. Frank still remained in his wheelchair and pointed to the chairs indicating they should sit.

"Frank," Marie began, "we have heard very little about you, but you are one of very few who has survived the severity of a stroke. I would like to write an article about you in the *Breeze* paper. Are you willing to do this?"

"Why not, I'm not going anywhere for a while." He spoke slowly with effort.

"Okay, I'll start with what happened and go back to your childhood where you were born and a few things like that."

He thought for a minute and then began at the beginning of his life. "I was told I was born in Detroit just off Woodward Avenue and left at the steps of a church. My adoptive parents were Angelica and Roberto Moreno. They owned a bakery. We lived upstairs above it. Before long, they owned another bakery and added more as each one became productive. By the time, I was twelve, they had me working after school, as well as getting up at three to help set the bread down to raise. I graduated from high school at Pershing High, with top honors and a scholarship to Michigan State. My father was disappointed because he wanted me to stay and help him with the business. I told him I would after I graduated because I would have a degree in business. He took it pretty well, and I entered college. I was proud to be on the dean's list and graduated four years later."

He fell back against the pillow, appeared to be exhausted.

Chapter Twenty
Big Man Talks

"Relax, Frank, you've been through a lot," Maria coached him.

"No, I want to get it out, it has to be told." He continued his narration. "I met a girl who was a freshman. So I traveled often to Lansing to see her, and when she graduated, we were married. Now I had a bakery to manage and a wife to manage too. She was a fiery one. Her parents were directly from Italy. Those brown eyes snapped, and I jumped.

"My dad and I had twelve bakeries by then, and we just pointed and said what we wanted. Don't get me wrong though, we did our share just to make sure our product was being done the same as it had all those years. My Cecilia and I were living in the best of style. We had a home in Gross Pointe Woods, we went to church every Sunday, and after a few years, we had two lovely girls, Rose and Alicia. I'll have to say the bakeries took up a lot of my time, so I would get tired and sleep somewhere besides my home. That was the beginning of the end of my marriage. She left after twenty years. I was forty-four, and she was forty. I sold my share of the bakeries to my father, and his new partner.

"I took my money and moved here. It's been almost twenty years, and I have lived simply in a home, not a mansion like we had. I stayed in my camp, a small cabin in the hard woods, and only went to my simple dwelling on the water when time allowed.

"Now here I am in a new home. I think that fire scared me. A lot of my money was sunk into the new skidder. I thought it would surely be burned up in that fire. We worked frantically to put it out, and we did.

"I'm getting older. After some rest, I'll be as good as new."

"What do you plan to do then?" Maria asked Frank.

"Go right back in the woods and keep on doing what I did before all this happened."

Maria finished writing and said, "Thank you. When I have this all compiled, I'll come back to talk to you and let you read what I have. If we need to change anything, I'll do it before I put it to print."

Frank smiled and said, "Thank you. I'm getting tired. I will see you when you have it ready."

"Okay, when I return, I'll get a picture of you for the article." Maria looked at her husband and they left the room. The nurse heard them open the door and quickly went in to adjust the bed and make him comfortable.

Later in the car George asked Maria, "What did you get from all that?"

"It was complete enough for an article, but I feel he was leaving something out."

"Hard to say, but I feel bad he has had a rough life yet still smiles."

George dropped Maria off at the news office and drove over to the mill where most of the timbered logs were sawed into lumber. The bark would be sold to locals for fire wood or crude décor siding. He had a hunch and needed information to back up his suspicions.

Frank had become a prime suspect with his sad story, and his recluse life away from his ex-wife and children. He believed Frank perhaps was hiding something from him after hearing his life story.

He turned off the road and drove up to the office, where he could see the owner, Mr. Chard, through the windows that revealed his yard out to the west.

"Good morning," Mr. Chard called out to George.

George took his hat off and shook Mr. Chard's hand. "Good afternoon, how's business?"

George looked down at the nameplate on Mr. Chard's desk. It read "William Marvin Chard." George recalled he didn't like being called by his first name, so he continued saying, "Mr. Chard."

"I can't complain. The trees keep coming in by the truckload."

George laughed. "I'm here to talk to you about a certain client of yours. His name is Frank Moreno."

"Ah, yes, he does send in some wood. As a matter of fact, he loads them on my truck when he has a load. He keeps the gaps filled, even though he only has the one woodsman cutting for him."

"I met his worker. He helped Frank when he had the stroke. He appeared to be a kind man to say the least."

"He has been working for Frank for around sixteen years. Yes, he seems to be amiable." Chard looked thoughtful then continued, "So what do you need to know about Frank?"

"Well, anything that will give me an idea what kind of person he really is. He told my wife, Maria, a very interesting story about his life before coming to the Upper Peninsula. My gut feelings are that he was leaving something out."

"All I know about his personal life is that he keeps to himself most of the time. He comes to pick up his check, he's always alone, and if he isn't staying in his little cabin on the ridge, he stays at the house on Cedarville Bay."

"So it's true he does have two dwellings. How does he contract his logs with you?"

"I find the acreage to be cleared off and subcontract it to him. It works pretty well, as I don't have the crew or time to do all of it."

"I see. What does he do, I wonder, while the help cuts the timber?" George thought out loud.

"That's a good question, George."

He has enough spare time to do other things that could relate to the actions in this area in the past few years, George thought. "I'm still working it out, thanks for your input." George headed for the door. "If you see anything unusual, please call me."

"Yes, George, I will. Have a good day."

Chapter Twenty-One
An Unusual Incident

Sharon was a young nurse assistant who began working at the rest home in Cedarville. She was raised on a farm north of Cedarville and had led a sheltered life. She was unsure about her duties, one to the other, lacking the self-confidence that most new hires have until they learn the routine.

She was willing and attempted to please her boss, Susan, the head nurse on nights. So far during her first week, Sharon was pleased to find none of the residents had complained as well as none of the workers.

While making her last rounds that particular night, she looked at the clock when it struck nine and realized she was almost done before the shift changed at ten. There were six rooms on the lower level of the convalescent home. Being a stroke victim, Frank was on this level. After working her way to the end of the hall, she knew she was almost finished for the day. She entered his room. Frank sat drooped in his wheel chair. His eyes lit up when Sharon entered the room. "Hello, Frank, it's time for you to go to bed. Here, let me help you." She helped him to his feet and swung him around onto the bed. Her arm was around his waist to help support him. He swung around and sat on the bed and began pulling her down with him. She struggled to get away. As she struggled, she discovered he had nothing on under his robe. He continued to use his good hand to push her face against his privates. She bit as hard as she could to get away from him, ending up with flesh in her mouth.

He screamed silently and grabbed his private parts while the blood flowed. She pushed the flesh in his mouth and ran from the room.

"Good night," Sharon called out to the other assistant as she left the building.

The next morning, the phone on the wall rang around six o'clock at George's home. "You need to come over here at the rest home as quick as possible, George."

"Who is this?" George asked.

"It's Gertrude, the head nurse at Cedar's Inn. We, the night nurse Susan and I, found one of the residents dead this morning a few minutes ago."

"Call Drake in St. Ignace, I'll be right over."

George arrived with the whole building all astir. Residents that knew about the death of Frank Moreno the stroke patient in a wheelchair, were whispering to each other at the breakfast table. Others were unaware because of their medical condition. One lady kept saying, "I don't want to be here, I don't want to be here," until one of the assistants said, "Here I'll take you to your room, Irene," while she helped her up to the women's wing.

George went to the nurse's station where he found Gertrude. "Good morning, Gertrude. Who has died that you need me?"

"It is Frank Moreno, the man you and Maria were talking to about a week ago. We suspect foul play."

"What? Shall you and I go down to Frank's room?"

"Yes, we didn't touch anything. It's just the way we found him."

"Good. Did you call Drake?"

"Yes, he's on his way."

The room was dark when they entered. Frank lay on the floor next to the bed in a pool of blood. George looked over the entire body as well as the room. Not a trace of blood beyond the circle of blood around his body existed.

George's radio signaled. He looked down to see the county sheriff's number pop up. He went to the main desk and dialed up the sheriff's office.

Chapter Twenty-Two
Double Trouble

"What is going on out there, George?" Chief Brown asked. "I just got a call from Jeffery Beacom, who found a dead girl on the road to Pickford. She hit a tree with her car and is dead. Her name is Sharon Wheatley. She apparently was on her way home from work or wherever. Jeffery said she was stiff and cold when he found her in the crashed car."

"I'll check it out as soon as I can. I'm busy with another death at the convalescent home in Cedarville. One of the residents has bled to death."

"Sorry to hear this. It seems you have your hands full, so I'll send out Deputy Paquin to check this accident out. Please join him when you're done there."

"Thanks, boss, I appreciate that, and I will meet with him as quickly as I wrap this up. Drake is on his way, so it won't be long."

"Good. I want a full report in my office as soon as possible."

"Yes, sir."

George was certain this was an unusual incident. Frank had only been living in the Cedar Inn for one week, and now he was dead. Bleeding to death from an uncertain and uncanny manner was beyond his imagination. How, why, and who were the questions that popped into his head.

"Glad you came right away, Drake. There's another death out on the road to Pickford."

"Was it an accident?"

"Yes, she drove into a tree."

George watched Drake go straight to his work. He heard George but kept his mind on what was at hand at the present.

"George, the other half of his male part was in his throat. He either did it himself or someone else was involved." Drake was talking to himself again, but this time he included George in his conversation.

"Brilliant deduction, Drake, this guy wasn't the type or didn't appear to be the kind to be strange. I do question some of his story about how he lived before he moved here so many years ago. I have to wrap my head around this for a few minutes to figure it out."

"Well, you'll have the time to do just that, once he's loaded into the hearse. I'm on my way back to the big city of St. Ignace. I'll leave you to your other duties here in the country."

"Quit giving me the cat's meow, Drake, I have to check out another body right up the road from here, and you'd better move him over to make room for her."

"I guess I am in the dark here. When and what are you talking about?"

"I thought you were listening when I told you about the accident. A girl has hit a tree and was found dead just an hour ago. The county sheriff called me to check it over after I was done here. I'm on my way there, so follow me over to the scene."

George jumped in his car while Drake pulled out after him and followed the three miles north to the scene. Jeffery and a nearby neighbor were seen waiting near the wreck.

"Hey, Jeffery, thanks for calling in for me. What time did you find her here?"

"I was driving to town this morning around seven thirty on my way to the café for breakfast. I saw the car smashed and crumpled against the tree, so I stopped to see if I could help. The second I reached for the door, I could tell she was dead. Her eyes were staring and glazed and her mouth gaped open. I went over to Hank Cory's here to call in for you. When Maria said you were busy on another case, I decided to call the county boys."

"Did you touch anything, Jeffery?"

"You know me better than that, George. I wouldn't no matter what. As soon as I saw she was dead, I left and have kept others from getting out of their car even though many drove by slowly."

"Thank you, I truly am grateful for your help, it has been a busy morning. Maybe you can help us get her out and on the stretcher here. Come on, Drake, we might as well get her in the hearse and send you on your way. I'll check the area out after you are gone."

Looking south as Drake drove away, George looked for anything to help decide why she hit the tree. No skid marks in the gravel indicated it wasn't a deer or a car that had crossed the middle of the road, unless it was a car and she merely veered to avoid hitting it. Still there wasn't any indication that she touched the brakes in the slightest. So she didn't put on the brakes. Maybe her brakes failed. She didn't smell of alcohol, so it appeared she had not been drinking. But Drake would make a positive report that would prove that. For now, he would have to say that she deliberately drove into the tree or her brakes failed. He would have Harry Thompson check the brakes when her car was taken by wrecker to his garage on the St. Ignace road. Then he could make a clear and final report. His primary report would only tell the facts as he saw them at the moment.

"I forgot to tell you, the radio was playing loudly when I stopped."

"Was the car still running, Jeffery?"

"Yes, but I turned it off."

"I thought you said you didn't touch anything."

"I'm sorry I forgot, but now I remember."

George took in a deep breath and let it out slowly. Jeffery was a help in spite of his being a real pain in the neck. *Help me, Lord,* George thought.

"All right, I understand. Thank you for remembering, Jeffery. Any detail you remember helps me do the investigation."

He radioed the main sheriff office in St. Ignace, "George here, please call Thompson's Garage to tell them I need him to pick up a car just north of Cedarville, about two and a half miles. I will stay here until he arrives."

The traffic was slow, but each car or truck that passed went slow and got a good look at the smashed car and the scrapes on the huge oak tree. George stood next to his car waiting. He kept the red lights flashing, so they would be aware and drive with caution. Soon the wrecker truck with Thompson's Garage written on the side along with his phone number below it arrived on the scene.

George signaled to the driver who proved to be Thompson himself. He backed up to the rear of the car and got out. He reached for the chain, pulled down on it while nodding a hello to George at the same time. He reached under the back bumper and hooked onto the frame, turned the hoist on and lifted the rear off the ground. The front tires were still full of air, so he pulled the car slowly out of the ditch and stopped.

"I'll check things out for you, George, and let you know what I find."

"Thanks, I need to know if the brakes were shot or anything else that could have caused her to fly into the tree. For example, it could have been a broken tie rod."

"Got it, George. It's all in a days' work." He looked at the tree with the bark peeled off where she hit it and shook his head. "She didn't make it, did she?"

"Nope, she didn't."

Chapter Twenty-Three
A Short Conversation

That night at the dinner table, George looked at his wife, Maria, his daughter, Susie, who was twelve now, and his son, George, who was six, and thanked God silently for his family. His thanks for the food was just a portion of his gratitude for all God had given him. His blessings erased the stress and sorrow he experienced that day.

"Daddy, do you know what I learned today in school? I learned that Eisenhower is thinking to run for president in the next election," Susie said.

"Now that's news, Susie. Do you suppose he's trying to beat FDR's record?"

Young George spoke up and said, "Eisenhower was a brave general, wasn't he, Dad?"

"He was a general, but I really couldn't say how brave he was because I never met him."

"George!" Maria scolded him.

They all laughed. It was good to be with family and eons away from the stark ways of life.

"The truth is, he has done a good job of being president and has the right to run again as much as any president has in the past. But Adali Stevenson is running, and he has a good reputation also."

"Hey, George, do you want Daddy to read you a nighttime story before you go to sleep tonight?"

"Oh, Dad, will you? I love the book *West of the Pecos* by Zane Grey, that's my favorite one."

"*West of the Pecos* it is then, George, and then to sleep." George winked over his young son's head to Maria and Susie.

"Dad, can I join you after we finish the dishes," Susie asked her father.

"Honey, go along with them, I'll do the dishes and follow when I'm done." Susie hugged Maria and went with the Georges for a good read. Maria inwardly smiled at the great evening they were sharing.

Sunday morning came soon enough, after a good rest. Maria was in the kitchen humming and preparing breakfast. The children were debating who would get in the bathroom first, and George thanked his Lord for thinking to clean up the night before. They would have a weekly family breakfast of bacon and eggs, before they attended church. Within an hour, they were on their way. They could hear the peal of the church bell as it rang the eighth hour. People were gathering together from their cars, trucks, and some walked to the sanctuary. The organ music could be heard from a distance, which enabled even those who weren't attending, become aware of the fact that somewhere there were people who loved to worship and give thanks for their blessings.

George, Maria, and family sat down in their usual pew. The organ music stopped as abruptly as it had started. The pastor began with announcements. The pancake supper would be on Friday night beginning at 5:00 p.m., the choir would practice after-church services, and the monthly elders meeting was scheduled for the usual second Tuesday night of the month at seven o'clock in the evening.

"We are sad to announce that Frank Moreno, one of our regular attendees, has passed away. There will be a funeral service here on Friday at eleven, followed with a meal served by the ladies of the church."

"Oh" was heard by the congregation, at which time George noticed that the woodsman, who brought Frank into the hospital two weeks prior looked shocked. He got up and left the church. George followed him.

"Excuse me, sir," George called to him.

He stopped and turned around. "Yes, what is it?"

"You appeared to be surprised to hear that Frank was dead."

"Surprised isn't the full description of how this news hit me. I knew he had a stroke and was recovering in the convalescent home, but I was not aware he died. I have continued cutting wood, and now I will be looking for work. I have no other means of income and the news is truly astounding."

Chapter Twenty-Four
Bleak Future

"I'm sorry to hear of your demise. Have you thought of going to the mill and asking Mr. Chard for work?"

"No, this is too fresh to think that fast. I'm going home and think what I must do next."

"Okay, sir, but I would go out to the mill when you have had time to think things over. Have a good day and keep in touch."

The damn fool! Doesn't he know that it's time for me to move on. I have nothing to keep me here now. Anna Belle looked at me strangely today in church, and it won't be long when she will recognize me and its curtains for me for sure, he thought.

When George reentered the church the pastor was telling of Sharon's funeral as well, which would be held on Saturday at eleven followed by a luncheon, and sadly, he asked for prayers for her family. He added that Frank Moreno had no living relatives.

Maria leaned over and whispered to George, "What about his ex-wife and children?"

"I'll check it out," George whispered back and nodded to pay attention to the pastor.

After church, they discussed the situation. "I'll talk about this with you, Maria, after the children are resting in their rooms," he said calmly. "They need not to know about the details."

Later after the children had their Sunday dinner, the biggest meal of the week, they went to their rooms.

Maria watched as they departed from the dining area then sat on the arm of George's chair and asked, "Now will you tell me what happened to Frank?"

"You remember his telling the story about how he and his wife separated?"

"Yes, I do, and I wrote it in his story. How he relocated and made a life of seclusion and profitable one with the timber business."

"Well, I have doubts about much of his story, so much so that I am thinking he was the serial killer of all the little girls so far. You see, Sharon died that night also. She either fell asleep or maybe a deer caused her to leave the road and hit a tree. Purely speculation, but it's a hunch, and after the examination by Drake and with the new man from Williamston, we should have more to go on."

"You haven't told me how Frank died."

"He bled to death. I don't know how it happened, but I am working on it."

"Oh, how terrible. He seemed to be such a nice man. What are the reasons you doubt his story?"

"He had a strange look when he told me about his former life, and especially what took place the day he had the stroke. There was a fire, and it made him very upset. I have reason to think something more happened that he kept silent about."

"You mean about why he was divorced or the fire?"

"Both. I plan on going out to the area where the fire was and take a second look tomorrow morning."

"I understand. Cross your t's and dot your i's."

"Yes, dear." He reached for her and gave her a loving hug.

"I also plan to check about the bakeries. Since he had no record of family, I'll have to check with legal records to discover if there is family left living. This will help me find if his wife and child or children are living."

Maria leaned in toward him and kissed his cheek. "Sounds like you have been doing your homework, George, and your day is full for tomorrow."

"But that doesn't mean we don't have time to enjoy ourselves the remaining part of today, does it?" He smacked her on the fanny.

* * * * *

The next morning brought rain, which allowed George to remain in the office making calls and finding out things.

By ten o'clock, he had good reason to believe Frank's story about the bakeries. Frank's family did have quite a chain of bakeries with a very good reputation for being the best in that area during their era. His father and mother had passed, leaving Frank and his children with the inheritance, which he had given to the children in escrow, until they became the age of twenty-five.

"Maria," he called across to his wife, "I do have evidence there is a family. Frank did have a family."

Maria rushed across with an eager look rising from her face. "How did you get it? Through the census or birth certificate records?"

"Yes, to both. I found that Cecilia, his wife, had remarried and the girls took their stepdad's name of Dumbrowski. Joe Dumbrowski and the family live in Hamtramck, the Polish district of Detroit. They still have one of the bakeries and have a restaurant along with it, serving kapusta, stuffed cabbage, and all the wonderful food that goes with it."

"Do you have an address and telephone number to go with this information?"

"I sure do, and I'm calling that number right away."

"Okay, I'll leave you to your business and return to mine, which is a follow-up to the story I wrote about Frank earlier."

"Honey, please don't do this until I know more about the investigation of his past."

"Sure, I'll hold it for now. I do understand, truly. I'm hoping that your suspicions are false. He seemed to be a nice man."

"Hello, this is George Kaughman from the Les Cheneaux area of the Upper Peninsula of Michigan. I'm calling to talk to anyone who knew Frank Moreno."

"I'm sorry, but he's out of my life, and I don't want to talk about anything concerning him," a woman's voice replied.

"Wait a moment, he has passed, and I understand he has children who may have inherited some of his possessions. There are two dwellings and his forestry equipment, possibly some contracts to fulfill or sell to an interested party."

"He's dead?"

"Yes, Cecilia, he had a stroke, and was living in a convalescent home here but died a week later." George kept the details from her for the time being.

"I'm sorry for the girls, they would have wanted to know, but it's over now, so I'll talk to their stepfather and my daughters. I'll get back with you, Sheriff George, as soon as I can," Cecilia said.

"I know this is difficult for you, but can you share with me what made you divorce him?"

"He worked all the time, and I…we never saw him. He would go to the bar and get drunk, then come home, fall on the couch or bed, and sleep until it was time to go back to the bakery at three in the morning. I had my fill, then he showed evidence he had been with another woman. That was it."

"I'm sorry, so please remember to call me back, Mrs. Dumbrowski, as soon as you have talked to the girls and your husband. Can I expect you to show for the funeral?"

"I will let you know after I have talked to my husband and the girls."

George thought for a minute after he hung up. Frank was a family man and risked losing what he had for a fast fun time? It's too bad he didn't have someone to guide him. But was he the kind to take advantage of a young girl? Was he thinking with a full deck? Was he a sick person? Did he change after he moved away from Detroit?

He stood up and slipped on his jacket, then poked his head into the news office. "Maria, I'm heading out to the place where Frank had his stroke. I'll be back in a couple hours."

Maria waved and smiled.

The drive was near twenty miles. He headed north to Pickford, then west out toward Rudyard. The drive brought him past the farm where Marjory lived. So far George had not found one clue as to where she had disappeared. He noticed when he drove by that neither parent was home. The place looked deserted. The grass hadn't been clipped or mowed. There wasn't a sign of use, such as laundry hanging on the clothesline. The windmill turned slowly in the slight breeze. The cattle looked up from grazing and mooed.

He drove past the end of the road turned west farther into the clearing where Ralph had the stroke. It had been timbered off. At the center there was a nice space where a homestead could be built. George noticed where the fire had spread through the grass and was put out by Frank and his woodsman, Matt Dillon. Matt had helped Frank to the hospital that day.

Did Frank have the stroke because he worried about the fire? He said he was worried that his logging machine would burn, but it stood clear from the fire area. George put the car in park and stepped out. He walked all around the burned-off edge, then moved closer to the center. He had picked up a branch that hadn't fully burned and began poking through the ashes, which had made a mound.

At first, he didn't notice much except what appeared to be unburned branches of the brush from the timber that had been cleared off. A closer look gave George a start. What he found was pieces of bone. Some were smaller and others were larger. He began to collect them in a pile. More digging surfaced the skull. That was when he discovered something shiny but dulled by the fire. It was a locket on a chain. Why didn't the killer notice it? Could it have been under her sweater? He paced in circles trying to get it straight in his head. How could anyone do this to a child? He picked up the chain and locket and put it in a bag he always kept in his pocket. He went to the trunk for a large evidence box to put the bones. They would have to be examined by Drake in St. Ignace. He looked at his pocket watch. It was near to three, which would put the time close for catching Drake before he left for the day.

Once George was out of the woods, he headed north on Pea Line, turned left on M-48 drove west to the road to Rudyard, but headed south instead in the direction of St. Ignace. He silently drove deep in thought and asked himself if this was the work of Frank Moreno? If it wasn't Frank, it had to be his worker. a man who attended church every Sunday. Most of the children loved to hang with him and talk about silly things that children would often do. He was so quiet yet smiled graciously at everyone. He always was willing to help when he was asked. He had helped his boss Frank even when he was deeply concerned about the fire as well as Frank collapsing and talking with a slur. Frank came first on Matt's list. Even with the fire still burning, as it had died down and he took Frank, his boss for immediate treatment.

How and why should it be Matt? Frank seemed to be the one, and Matt came to help Frank burn the brush. That had to be it.

"Drake, I have a couple items to be seen here. I went out to the timber stand where Frank Moreno had the stroke. I found bones in the smoldering ashes that appear to be human. I want you to verify my hunch. They could possibly be those of Marjory, the little girl that came up missing from the Pea Line road where the timber stand leads out."

"What? Oh, no, I hope you're wrong. Has anyone said she is still missing? She didn't come home yet?"

"No, and the folks there haven't been around each time I have went over. I'm not sure if they work away or are being scarce. It's a funny scene. The cows seem to be all right, plenty of grass, hay, and water. But the lawn hasn't been cut, nor are there any fresh tracks each time I go over there."

"I'll get right on this as soon as I can. I just got the results in from Frank's corpse, and the young woman Sharon."

"Good."

"Let's see here, Frank had bitten off his…you know and bled to death, or so it appeared. He was found on the floor, as though he tried to get help and fell when he tried to get up out of the wheel-chair. The flesh was still in his mouth, he choked on it. I believe he was dead before all his blood drained from him."

"What, he had a seizure, which caused it?" George asked.

"I believe he could have."

George had his hand over his mouth with a thoughtful expression.

"What did you find with the woman, Sharon?"

"She took a dive off the edge of the road. She was going at a speed of at least fifty or more. There were no brake tracks, so she was thought to have passed out or fallen asleep."

"Or deliberately did it?" George asked.

"Okay, here's what we found. Her blood was everywhere on her clothing, from the gash on her forehead. The abrupt crash into the maple tree caused a terrible force. The collision caused immediate death or very shortly afterward. The puzzle is that there was a second type of blood on her shirt. Not her own. We have come to the conclusion that, she got the blood from—"

"Frank," George interrupted. It was what he feared but didn't want to believe.

Drake waited for George to say more but realized he was waiting for more information from him. "Yes, it was Frank's blood."

Chapter Twenty-Five
Reading of the Will

The funeral for Frank was fast and brief. As far as family goes, no one showed up except his ex-wife and the two daughters. No one cried but the family had plenty of questions about the two homes and his personal property afterward.

Matt Dillon sat in the rear, nodded to George and his family. There were a few members from the congregation who showed up out of respect. The ladies prepared a luncheon of sandwiches, pickles, and deserts. They had prepared hot coffee and iced tea to drink after the service.

Matt left without eating. Cecilia Dumbrowski and the daughters, Rose and Alicia stayed to eat and asked about his life in the Upper Peninsula.

"He stayed near the timber which grew along the ridge from Cedarville area to as far as Rudyard. He had a small cabin made of logs. I can take you out there if you wish."

"And the other house is near the bay?"

"Sure, we can go to both. The girls may want to take a swim while there. He had a very nice beach out away across a healthy lawn from the house."

The fat head, Cecilia thought, *he insists on calling my daughters the girls. They are well over the age that you refer to them as girls. Rose is sixteen and Alicia is near eighteen.*

They headed out to the cabin first, probably to see the best home of the two last.

Approximately an hour later, they arrived at the cabin in George's car. The yard was neat with a stone walk leading to the front door. A well pump stood near the door just off the front porch. He opened the creaking door to Frank's one room shelter. There was a bed in one corner, a small fireplace on the opposite wall, a table with two chairs, a cupboard with a small amount of food and dishes.

"How he stayed in this is beyond me. He gave up an awful lot for this." She waved her hand over the entire area.

"It is meager but sufficient for what he used it for," George offered.

"I suppose," Cecilia said. The girls remained silent and made no comment.

"Well, I hope his other home is a bit better than this one is." She sniffed.

"Let's go and see." George knew what Frank's home looked like but also knew that her comments would be exactly what she thought and she wouldn't spare anyone's feelings. He also thought that Frank must have been half relieved to get away from her. After all, where was Mr. Dumbrowski today?

They drove back to Cedarville and along the water that curved along the point to the left. George drove up to Frank's home that was sitting facing the bay from his front room. They entered from the south end of the home, which entered into a kitchen and extended twenty feet to the dining room with a round oak table accompanied with six chairs to match and an open two story living room. The fireplace was the full two stories high. The opposite wall had an open staircase, which led to three bedrooms and a bath, directly above the one off the dining room.

Cecilia was speechless. "I can't imagine what he needed such a big home for."

"Let's go out on the front porch to enjoy the view," George remarked. "You girls want to take a swim?"

"No!" Cecilia screamed at the same time the girls said, "Yes!"

"There's a changing room in the boat house over there to your left. He has spare suits for you in there." George had already viewed the entire location when he checked the place right after Frank's death.

The girls response made George chuckle, while it certainly caused discomfort for their mother.

"Humph," she said. "I guess I'll have to sit here and watch them enjoy themselves."

"Yes, so tell me all about what you remember of Frank."

125

"He was a hard worker, but we had a much nicer home than this. He had a mansion built for me and the girls. In Gross Pointe Woods, you know, where all the millionaires live?"

"No, I didn't know that."

"Yes, so we had everything, and he gave it all up for that… I won't call her a bad name, but it ended our marriage of twenty years. He seemed to like younger women, much younger, if you know what I mean. She wasn't much older than my two daughters."

"Do you still live in the home he provided for you?' George asked her, while he made a mental note about the age of Frank's mistress.

"No, we live in another home that is as nice and in a better location. I'm happy with him, and he has been a good father to the girls. We have two other children, boys that will carry on his name."

"I'm happy for you, Cecilia, but I still haven't figured out one thing. What his private life was and what you plan to do with the estate."

"That's two things. As for the house, I'll take the steps to have it put in my two daughter's name. They can decide what they want to do with it when they are of age."

"Okay, that is a good decision. And the remaining items, the cabin and skidder?"

"Give them to the worker if he wants them, or he can sell them, it's up to him."

"We will have to draw up legal papers to that effect. Can you stay another day to do this?"

"Yes, then we will leave this forsaken place once and for all," Cecilia huffed.

George cleared his throat. "I understand how you feel." But he really didn't because he loved it in this region of the world. However, she being a city girl helped him to realize her feelings.

"So then, George, you will meet with us at the lawyer's office tomorrow in St. Ignace as a witness to the dispensing of the will?"

"As I said, I will be happy to do you this favor. I'm sure your daughters will be pleased to have a part of their dad's belongings so they can relate to their true blood and know him a little more. Shall

I tell Matt Dillon that he should be there for the reading of the will also?"

"I suppose, if that's the natural thing to do," Cecilia, Frank's ex-wife, slowly replied.

"All right, I'll go out there this afternoon to let him know, so he can be ready to attend the reading."

"My appointment is precisely at two in the afternoon, so we will expect he will be there at that time as well," Cecilia stated.

The very next day, Cecilia and her daughters left for St. Ignace to sign papers. The trio arrived early, only to discover that Mr. Brown had left for lunch at twelve and had not returned yet. The secretary told them they could wait in the reception room or do some window-shopping to spend the time until two o'clock.

Cecilia Dumbrowski was in a huff, so her daughters were to calm her down by saying they had seen a nice museum on their way along N. Street on the bay side. They had at least forty-five minutes to kill until the appointment. "I'd rather drive back to the museum as walking wears the stompers out."

They climbed into their 1956 Pontiac, a sleek two-tone black and white, and drove back to the museum. The artifacts were of the Native Americans who dwelt there early in the history of the settlement of St. Ignace. The artifacts were of old clay bowls, crocks, and handmade tools of that era. There was some very intricately made jewelry as well as a war bonnet worn by the chief at that time. Father Marquette had settled there as well, later in the history, so many of his clothing, beads, and Bible sat with history of his communication with the native population and how they were impressed with his ways, religion, and newness from a foreign land. The primitive plows, tools, and way of life was a delight to at least Alicia, if not Rose as well. As for Cecilia, she could care less, or so it appeared to the girls.

"I wonder if that 'chrome dome' has arrived yet. I'm not impressed with his ready smile and gleaming eyes."

"How do you know he's bald, Mom?"

"He scratched his dirty, oily head. I saw it when he lifted his hat to scratch it."

When they parked next to the curb in front of the attorney's offices, they noticed that George was already there, as well as the "chrome dome." He must have rode in with George.

Finally the secretary told the five that they could go in to the main office to talk to Mr. Brown.

Mr. Brown shook hands and cleared his throat before beginning to read the will.

"I, Frank Moreno, being of sound mind and have clearly decided to disburse with my personal property for the good of my family, friends, and acquaintances in the following way. First, I wish to leave the main house to my daughters, Rose and Alicia. This will include all the furniture and personal items. And finally my two daughters, Rose and Alicia, will inherit my share of the bakery line. It will be held in escarole, as each reach the age of twenty–five. They may dispense them as they see fit. The cabin in the woods and my skidder will be given to my worker, Matthew Dillon, who has been a loyal and hard worker for these many years."

Matt had a very surprised look on his face and so did Cecilia. Once again, Frank had taken her joy away. She wanted to be the established donor. She wanted to wear that crown.

Mr. Brown continued, "If there is any conflict to this statement, and vow, by Frank Moreno, it has very little pliability, so documented by Frank Moreno on this date of September 12, 1953."

As everything appeared to be said, Mr. Brown asked the three to sign the papers to prove they accepted the will as read. He asked his secretary and George to witness their signatures, and they were given each a copy of the document for further use to legalize the ownership of each item.

"Time to take a powder," Cecilia said, as she rushed the girls into the Pontiac and said goodbye to George, nodded to Matt, and departed for Detroit.

"She sure talks funny," Matt said.

"She's from the big city." George laughed.

Chapter Twenty-Six
A New Day

By eleven, the people from all areas came and filled the church. Sharon had so many bouquets and floral arrangements around her, that some had to be lined against the walls on either side. As shy as she was, many liked her and were close with the family. Her final sermon lasted over an hour. Many followed to the Cottle Cemetery, just west of Pickford about four miles, where her remains were buried.

The entourage drove silently through cedars, then hard woods to the top of Rock View where they could see the valley where Pickford is located. Productive rich farmland spreads to each side as far as the cedar swamps to the east and the hardwoods to the west toward Rudyard. The day turned out sunny and warm along with a slight breeze, which was refreshing to those who were adapted to the cold winters and felt warmer than "trolls" who had transplanted from Lower Michigan and needed the warmth.

The graveside service was short. George looked around the crowd where he noticed the parents and family crying, her friends looking down at the ground, some smiling assurance to others, and a few strangers who felt it necessary to attend.

No one present showed anything suspicious to George. He observed everyone in case she had talked to anyone about her experience. It was just as well. Frank might have "snapped his cap," as Cecilia would say, if Sharon had anything to do with his death.

The women had prepared a full dinner of turkey, stuffing, potatoes, and all the trimmings. As the mourners returned they filled the dining area and some went out on the veranda to enjoy food and visiting. It seemed festive, in spite of her loss, many including the family, mom, and dad wanted it that way, so the memory would not be forgotten and they would know they gave Sharon a good send off.

One car full at a time slowly parted for home, to do chores or other tasks toward evening. A full day was enjoyed by most of the partakers of this event.

Monday followed the weekend in a slower pace. George decided to get out and talk to Garde. Jeffery Beacom had talked to George at the funeral when they were at the cemetery. Jeffery told George the answers he need to know about the three men in question. Maxwell did have a small cabin on the mainland, which was near town across from the Snow's Channel. Andre Toulose hunted and made crafts to sell, which made him a modest income and kept him from needing money for survival. As for Garde Kengas, he received a disability check monthly from the government. He was injured when his father was killed as a tree fell on his dad. George recalled smiling inward at Jeffery who was out of breath after telling all his information without breathing.

George's schedule was so packed for some time, and he knew today was a good day to check this man out. Garde was of Norwegian descent, a tall man who had a very light complexion and rosy cheeks. His eyes were the color blue of a fine summer sky. He wore a flat cap with small visor, high waist pants with brown suspenders. Today he wore long johns on top without a flannel shirt. He stepped off his low porch and greeted George as he approached.

"Hello."

George reached out and shook Garde's hand. "I'm the local deputy sheriff from Cedarville, George Kaughman."

"I've seen you around but have never met you, George. However, I have heard good things about you."

"Thank you," George replied. "I have wanted to come out and meet you for quite some time. Since you don't come to town often, I decided to come out and make an acquaintance."

"As you can see, I live here alone and spend most of my time trapping or hunting. I keep to myself most of the time and only come to town when I need supplies, including ammo and traps," he said to George. "Come in I'll show you some of my pelts and artwork."

George obliged and was awestruck to see lamps made with fur pelts, bear rugs in front of the divan and fireplace. The home was immaculate with a museum like appearance. George couldn't see anything to make this man possibly be a mutilating butcher.

Their conversation led George to say, "Come in and visit the church sometime. I'm sure you would like it."

Garde smiled and waved at George without giving an answer.

As he drove toward home, George mulled over the conversation he had with Garde and shook his head. This man was not even close to a suspect. However, appearances could be deceiving. George observed that Garde had difficulty breathing. He either had allergies or asthma. As Garde talked, his mouth hung open. He gasped between words as he grunted out his words depraving him of his breath.

Chapter Twenty-Seven
Susan Missing

One evening, few days later that week, George and Maria settled down for the night. They put George to bed and wondered when Susie's Uncle Fredrick and his wife, Penny, would bring their daughter back. George called the farm.

"Hey, when are you bringing Susie home?"

"Susie isn't here. She didn't come after school. Isn't she there?"

"No, and I'm worried. I'll have to let you go so I can check to see if she is somewhere with her girlfriend and their family."

Maria looked worried. "She didn't go out there on the bus?"

"No, Maria, we will have to check with Rose's family."

Maria called immediately, as George sat on the edge of his seat. "They aren't answering, George."

"Call the school principal's home. He may know where she went."

Maria handed the phone to George. "Mr. Greeley, did you see Susie leave school today? She didn't go out to the farm and her friend Rose's family isn't answering the phone either. I'm hoping you saw where she went or who she went with."

"I did see her go with a man, she seemed to know him. I didn't think anything about it."

"Man, this is my daughter you're talking about. She would never go with someone. We've taught her better than that. Was there anyone else in the car?"

"I didn't see anyone else. Not that I noticed."

"What color was the car?"

"Did I say car? I meant truck."

"She got in a truck? What color?"

"Green, it looked green."

"What make and model?"

"I think it was a Ford, or no, maybe a Chevy. I'm sorry, I'm not sure."

"Was there anyone there to see her go with him?"

"Sure, the whole school left after school. Calm down, George. It's not like she is dead or something. She'll come along soon, I'm sure of it."

"You ignorant fool, what a thing to say to the child's parent." Maria took the phone and said, "Mr. Greeley what has made my husband talk to you like that?"

"He said she wasn't dead, and we shouldn't be worrying, to calm down," George said loudly.

"Maria, I just think George was overacting, and I was trying to calm him down."

"Thank you, Mr. Greeley, we'll call some of her friends to see if they saw her."

George took the phone and called the county sheriff's office. They immediately put on alert for anyone possibly having a thirteen-year-old girl with them and warned to watch for any kind of suspicious action. He told the story about his daughter not coming home from school, and now it was past her bedtime.

Maria asked George if he knew what she may have done to think they would not worry about her.

"I can't think of anything. She knows she is supposed to let us know where she is or ask us if she can spend time with one of her friends."

"I'll try her friend's home again." She reached for the phone where it sat in its cradle. "No answer."

"Who does she chum with?"

"That Brenner girl, but, I told her not to go with her because of her reputation. Mr. Brenner spends most of his time in the bar and his wife does all the work, milking cows. Patty is Susie's age and all four boys are older," Maria said.

George interrupted, "I have had to talk to the boys before because they were drunk, like their father, and they were driving all over the road when I stopped them."

"George, please don't get all torn up, we need to pray Susie is all right. Our Heavenly Father will take good care of her."

"You're right, Maria, let's pray."

Their heads were bowed and they held hands, when they heard a truck drive up. Susie came in with the happiest smile on her face. "Hi, Mom and Daddy, I've been shopping in Sault Ste. Marie with my friend Rose and her mom and dad. I'm sorry it took so long, but we had a flat tire and had to fix it."

They were so happy to see her that they just hugged her and said they were happy that she got home safely.

"Look, Mom, I even got some mountain candy for you because you love them so much. Only four though."

Maria held back tears and hugged her again. George thanked the Lord she was safe.

All the thoughts that traveled through his mind in just a short few hours were devastating enough so that George was sure the serial killer was back from the dead and was assaulting his little girl. He was so thankful to find she was just shopping.

All the girls who were missing or dead in the past seven years all flashed across his mind. Jenny Adams, the girl found in the ditch; an unknown female's bones found by a dog; Hanna Franklin, a girl from Swede road, missing but never found; Anna Belle Carter, a girl who was missing but found in the woods in a hollow log in a coma; Marjory Sharp, from Pea Line Road; then Sharon, who hit a tree and was killed. Six were dead or missing. Was it Frank Moreno? Did he go wacko and preyed on helpless young girls? Who was this sociopath that lurked in the shadows?

If it was Frank, it would be a relief to George. He had struggled with who it could have been for these past years from the first little Jenny. She came to the window each time he had passed by the haunted old farm. He made sure to plan to go over there in the morning. Just before falling asleep, he thanked his Heavenly Father again for his family and Susan's safe return home. He felt truly blessed and filled with relief.

The population at the school was just over one hundred students. By the time Susie came to her first class, everyone knew she had played hooky on her parents. Her friends teased her and others, the adults, talked behind her back saying she was a naughty girl. Susie took everything like a grain of sand. She knew she had not done anything bad, and she was safe from being sought out by the predator.

Deep down she knew she had worried her parents, and the last thing she wanted to do was worry them. If this ever happened again, she wouldn't go with Rose, unless her parents knew where she was.

Chapter Twenty-Eight
At the Quarry

A week later, the quarry boss called George to tell about a discovery at the piles of small peastones.

"I'm calling to tell you that one of the operators was filling a dump truck of peastones when he saw what looked like the remains of an animal. He got off the front end loader to take a closer look, when he realized it was a human skeleton. A small body, which appeared to be a girl, because of the clothing that had not rotted from the length of time it had been buried. George, the first thing I thought I should do is to call you. Then if you want to call whoever you think, it's up to you."

"I'll be right out there, Ben. I will contact Drake first so he can get there before we call the parents of missing children or whoever I find this body to be."

"Drake, here, how may I help you?"

"It's George, the quarry boss just called. His operator found a body."

"I'll be right out. Which area did they find it?"

"It was just off the road to the left as you're coming east. They said it was in the small peastone piles."

"Okay, I'll see you there."

George set out to get there as soon as he could because he had to be sure who it was before making any decisions. Drake would be all business as usual when he is upset about a young one, which was George's hunch. It no doubt was the Franklin girl, unless he killed someone that no one reported to him about. Fifteen minutes later, he drove into the yard. The yellow-orange loader sat next to the piles of peastones. Ben and the loader operator Dan was standing there talking and pointing here and there.

"Hello, Dan, sorry we have to be seeing each other under these circumstances, but duty calls us more often than a good beer at the Cedarville Bar."

"You'll need a handkerchief, George, the body is pretty ripe. We think it is a girl. Possible the one that was missing a few months back."

"Let's take a look," George said.

All three walked the short distance to the freshly dug peastones that revealed the girl's remains. Part of the flesh had decayed, however, her clothing was still recognizable for her parents to identify her.

George shook his head when he saw her clothing was ripped off. There was no evidence that her undergarments were present. Both her shoes were still on her feet. A ribbon emerged with the loose stones. George was sure this would be enough for her parents to say yes or no.

"Ben. I'll need your phone to call the family."

"Jump into my truck, and I'll drive you up to my office. Dan, move on down to the next pile to get your stones. Make sure there isn't anything in your scoop that should be used for evidence."

"Thanks, Ben. You're right. He should empty the front scoop in case there is anything, like part of her body or clothing. It's a shame to find that she is dead, and here we were looking for her, hoping she was alive all along. Finding her sure will be hard on her parents. They won't take this too easily."

Ben drove to the main road, waited for an oncoming car, then went across to the office.

A name plate next to the phone, carved in marble, said Benjamin Slater. George dialed the Franklin home. "Hello, this is Sheriff George I need you and your husband to meet me at the quarry office. We think we have found your daughter and will need positive identification."

"She is dead?"

"Yes, I'm sorry, Rose. She is dead."

"I feared that, but now..." George heard her weep and suck in to continue talking. "I'll have to get my husband, he's milking the cows. We'll be along as quick as he is finished. I'll help him so we can get there as quickly as we can."

"No need to hurry. I'll be here and will wait until you come before Drake takes her to the morgue for examination." George felt sick for her. "I'm sorry that you have to go through this. I know how you are feeling right now."

"It's all right, we knew that she wasn't coming back, but we didn't know how long it would be before we knew for sure if she was dead or alive." Her voice broke, and George knew for sure she was crying this time. She couldn't stop.

"I'll see you when you get here."

"Ben, this is the hardest part of my job. I like upholding the law. It's an everyday routine, but when I see the hurt and the anxiety family or friends go through, it's all I can do to not show my compassion for their feelings."

"I have no doubt about that, George. You do a great job. I'll never forget about your friend Two Shoes being murdered, and the fact that he was your lifelong friend. Many have said you held up and solved the crime in spite of your emotions."

"I can thank the man upstairs for that. Let's get back to the discovery site."

"Yes, of course. You take my truck. I'll stay until Rose and Pete Wheatley get here. I can ride over with them."

The quarry yard was entirely made of calcite and peastones, leaving a beautiful sight of white against the blue waters of Lake Huron and the true green of cedar. The short drive back across the main road to the place where Dan remained until they returned didn't take more than five to six minutes. George could see that Drake wasn't there yet. He knew the Wheatleys would be there as soon as they had finished the milking but was surprised when they arrived only a half hour later, still in their barn clothing.

George stepped up to greet them and warned of the odor of the decadent flesh. They wouldn't listen because they were eager to believe it may not be Hanna Franklin and wanted to prove it in their mind and heart.

"Listen, you may want something to cover your face, especially your nose, because the body has decayed and has a strong odor at this time," George told them.

"Oh, I never thought of that," Rose said.

"Here, honey, take my kerchief," her husband, Pete, said.

The Franklins followed George the short distance to where the remains were laid, waiting for Drake to come to examine and take her to the morgue.

Grace gasped. "It's her. I would recognize her skirt any time. I sewed it for her from material she picked out at Penney's in Sault Ste. Marie."

"Look closely, Rose. You too, Pete. We must be accurate in your witness. Is there anything else that indicates she is your daughter?"

As hard as it was for them to not feel what she went through, they calmed down and looked for any trace of anything that would make an accurate report to identify their daughter. The body was near totally decayed. They needed to find something else there to help them recognize her. "There it is. She wore an ankle bracelet, and there it is lying on the ground near one of her leg bones," Rose sobbed out.

"The shoes are ones we bought for her for Christmas. That may help too," Pete added.

Rose was hanging on to Pete, sobbing against his chest. "The poor dear darling, what she must have suffered. You must find him, George, and give him life in prison. He doesn't deserve to live. Let him rot in Marquette State Prison."

"There, there, sweetheart, I know what you're feeling. I am also. She was the sunshine of my heart."

Drake drove up and witnessed the parents hugging and Rose sobbing. He waited for them to notice he had arrived.

George introduced the parents, Rose and Pete Wheatley, to Drake.

"George, can I have her ankle bracelet?"

"Yes, after the investigation and court hearing. We will need it for evidence."

They looked at each other, excused themselves, and left. George realized they didn't want to see their daughter's body scraped into a body bag.

George put the shoes into an evidence bag and the ankle bracelet into a smaller one.

Drake unzipped the black body bag while Dan put the front end loader up close to the body parts. He waited while Drake and George placed everything possible into the scoop. Then Dan slowly rolled the body and parts into the bag.

"I've got to say, George, you have your hands full here. Please catch this bugger before he hits again."

"I just crossed another suspect off my list. That narrows it down. It'll be soon."

Drake drove away without saying one more thing. He looked in the rear window mirror and waved.

George nodded at Dan, the loader operator, and left with the evidence placed safely in his trunk.

He had one stop before he returned to his office. It was at Maxwell Stewart's home on the Little LaSalle Island.

He stopped at the office at the boat rental and looked for the manager. No one was around. He stepped off the porch and headed out to the boats, tugged on the starter string, and jumped in the boat after the first pull and a running motor.

Once docked on the spot where Max parked his boat, he tied it to a dock post and advanced toward the house. He knew he was going to have fun trying to talk to him, so he remained outside. He didn't need a thud on the head again anytime soon.

"Hello, in the house." He cupped his hands around his mouth so his voice projected and became louder. No answer.

"Hello, in the house," he called again.

"What do you want?" the voice of Max called back.

"I need to talk to you, Max. We found the girl that I asked you about."

"You don't say. Well, I've been busy this last week. I married the girl of my life. We've been honeymooning."

"All I want to ask is where you were the night Hanna came up missing. Can you answer that now?"

Max stepped out of the foyer onto the rock path and faced George. "I was busy with my girlfriend. I didn't want you to know about her because we eloped. Her parents took it grand, and all is well now, but before it was a secret. Claudia, come out here," he called into the house.

Claudia shyly came out and gave George a slow smile. "Hello."

"Claudia wants to say she is sorry for hitting you on the head that day when you entered the house in the dark."

"Yes," she said, "I am sorry, but I didn't know who you were. As Max said, we were trying to keep our plans a secret."

George reached out and shook her hand. "I guess in that case, I'll accept your apology. So you testify that you were with Max the night Hanna came up missing? I'll need you to take an oath that you were with Max that night in court when I find the culprit."

"I sure will," she answered then smiled.

* * * * *

George drove up to the news office and his, which was two offices in one building, where his sign read "Local Deputy Sheriff Office" next to the large words "The Wave, Your Weekly Newspaper."

He removed the evidence from the trunk and entered his office, placed it on his desk, and began to examine the shoes first. He immediately saw that there was sand in the cracks of her saddle shoes. The quarry was totally limestone and other white powdered minerals. This indicated she was picked up on a sandy road before ending up at the quarry. He wrote this discovery on a note and kept it in the evidence bag. Another note was made in his private notes, dated as well and stored in a locked drawer in his desk.

Next he examined the ankle bracelet. He couldn't see much there except a possible piece of flesh that could have been yanked off her leg by the perpetrator, as he snatched it off her leg and threw it to the spot where George found it.

He took the flesh off and placed it in a small vile with the solution Drake had given him. He would take this in for evidence to compare with Hanna's other flesh. Drake would know how to do this procedure.

He suddenly realized he was tired and needed to go home. This was a full day with much to do the next day.

* * * * *

It was time to check out the men he had suspected prior to finding Hanna. She was the final blow to his thoughts. However, Max could still have been the guilty one and his sweetheart was lying for him.

Chapter Twenty-Nine
Chet Takes a Ride

Chet was home when he arrived. He answered the door by asking, "What are you here for?"

"I'd like you to go for a ride with me, Chet, if you have the time. I'm thinking about those girls that have been murdered in the last few years with no clue. Maybe you can tell me something after we take a ride to the quarry and back around via Webb Road."

"Well, I'm sure not going to know anything more than I did the last time you stopped over, but if it will make you feel better I'll go along with you. You're lucky that you found me home. I have all my work caught up and now I do have the time to go along with you."

Back in the car, George headed out Swede Road toward the quarry. He silently watched Chet and his expressions as they went past the Franklin farm. George noticed that Charles was out in the field working with his John Deere tractor and equipment of some sort. "Yeah, you know, this is the farmer that, his daughter was found in the quarry, buried under the stones there," Chet blurted out.

"How did you know this, Chet?"

"Everyone's talking about it. They say she was rotted off the bones, and the only way they could identify her was her shoes and leg bracelet. If I was the killer, I would have taken it off her."

George looked at him and relaxed some. If he was the killer, he would have known that it was removed and thrown away from her in the other direction. On the other hand, if he was the killer, he would act as though he didn't know about it, to throw suspicion on to someone else.

"Do you want to see the spot where she was found?"

"Not especially. Why? Are you going over to that spot?"

"I'm headed that way right now. Thought I'd double check the area around where she was found."

143

"Don't you suppose the area is tainted by now after everyone knows about it?"

"Possible, but I'm going out there anyway."

George pulled up near the area where they found Hanna next to the peastones and stopped. He got out and called across to Chet, "Come on out and stretch your legs, Chet."

Chet acted as though he was going to see a ghost. "Okay, if you insist. I can't for the life of me understand why you're hanging around looking at the death areas."

"Who knows, Chet, something may pop up."

"That's what I was thinking."

George looked closely once again throughout the area for anything that he missed a couple of days prior. Maybe a piece of metal from the vehicle or her personal item he wasn't sure what he may find. He shuffled around and finally did discover a piece of a rusted fender, which had very little paint on it. It could be from someone parking out there or a hunter or the killer. George picked it up and dropped it into an evidence bag. The paint appeared to be green.

* * * * *

Soon they were going past the sandy road where the dog found the bones of an unknown small woman or girl. Chet was acting nervous. "What are we doing here?"

"I'm just checking to see if my friend Matt is home." As they passed by his place, George said, "Looks like he isn't. Have you ever been down this road, Chet?"

"Can't say as I have, I don't recall. All these back roads look the same, all trees and sand."

George noticed he began to get antsy and couldn't set still in his seat.

"You want to get out and stretch your legs, Chet?"

"Oh, no, I'm fine."

George went onward for three and a half miles, winding and turning when he was near the Carter farm. "Do you know who lives here, Chet?"

"No, I don't, but I believe you're going to tell me."

"Not necessarily, I just wondered if you did."

They kept traveling beyond the Carter property. They passed the Catolica farm, where Bill's wife, Vincenza Catolica, baked every day for her Bill and the local restaurants. George turned around the corner and off the Webb Road on another sandy road where George slowed almost to a creeping speed. He looked up at the window in the deserted Miller farm to see if Jenny looked back at him, but there was no sight of her.

"Ever been over this way before, Chet?"

"No, but you can keep going. Did you see what I saw in the window? It was a shadow or a ghost looking out at me. Drive faster, let's get away from here." George noticed he didn't look in the direction where George had carried little Jenny to the stretcher with Drake.

"Let's head back. Would you like to stop at the Runway Bar for a beer before we return?"

"Sounds like a good idea."

Twenty minutes later, they walked into the Runway Bar, slid on a stool, and heard the bartender ask, "What will you have, boys?" She saw George and said, "Sorry, George, I didn't realize it was you."

"We'll have a beer on tap."

"Would you like Miller or Bud?"

"I will take a Miller, and what for you, Chet?"

"Bud thanks."

They noticed there were several people seated or playing pool. Most were men although there were a couple of women. Then George spotted Rob Lightfoot. He wore his official reservation cop uniform. "Hey, partner, how is everything in your neck of the woods?"

"Are you being facetious or joking?" Rob asked him.

"I'm just glad to see you. It's been some time since you and I had a good talk."

"Not today, but I do want to see you very soon. There is a situation that we need to talk about."

"What about tomorrow morning, here or at my office, Rob?"

"Here or at my place will be good. It is good to see you, George. You're looking good in spite of your daily chores. Seems the wife is taking good care of you, and the children?"

"They are good too. Susie is thirteen now and little George is seven. They keep me busy with sports and my reading George segments of Zane Grey every night if I am home before he goes to bed, which is more often than not."

"So he likes western stories?"

"He sure does. Do you know Chet here? He works on Mackinaw Island."

"Howdy, Chet, it's nice to meet you."

Chet extended his hand, and they shook hands, smiling at each other.

"Can I buy you two another?" Rob asked.

"One more won't hurt before we leave for home."

Chet looked at George and was grateful, as he really was shaken to see a ghost.

After they finished the drink, Lightfoot had purchased for the two George said, "See you in the morning, Lightfoot."

When George dropped off Chet, he never looked back as he headed to his home with a hand raised in a goodbye.

* * * * *

That evening was humorous for George. Little George was all wound up about a field trip he had gone on with his teacher and class to find rocks, birds, and wildflowers. They took a ride out along the Lake Huron shore, parked, and walked the trails searching for the three items the teacher had told them about.

"And that's when Ronnie had to go to the bathroom. He filled his pants. Everyone was laughing at him, Dad, and I felt sorry for him, but I laughed too," George reported. "The next thing I know, Carolyn was reaching for a flower that was growing next to the creek and fell in the water. She almost drowned. Mrs. Goodman had to reach out to her with a long stick, and she lost her balance and almost fell in too."

"What did Mrs. Goodman do about Ronnie?" George asked his son.

"Oh, she had him take off his underpants and blue jeans. She took the underwear and washed them in the creek and hung them on a bush. Ronnie cleaned up and put just his jeans on until his under garment dried. But, Dad, you should have seen the look on Mrs. Goodman's face when she almost fell in the creek too. All of us laughed so hard. She looked mad but laughed with us after she got Carolyn out of the water."

"I'll bet she was having a really eventful day. Did you get the rocks and flowers and see many birds?"

"Lots of rocks, but not many flowers after Carolyn almost fell in the water. We did see a 'kill deer,' at least that's what the teacher called it. Because it keeps saying 'Kill deer, kill deer,' sounds just like it."

"Son, you really did have a great day."

"Yeah, Dad, I'm too tired tonight to hear you read Zane Grey. I'm just going to do my homework and go to sleep."

George ruffled his hair and laughed, "Okay, son, I'll check on you when I go to bed."

Maria chuckled all the while she listened to the conversation between father and son. Their evenings were always special, one way or another. Even Susie was enjoying George's experience and how he related it to the family.

She kissed her mom and dad and said, "Good night, I'm headed to my room too. See you both in the morning."

George looked at how mature she was becoming and said proudly to his wife, "Maria, we have two wonderful children, and Susie is growing into a young lady. They and you make me so happy, I can't be more blessed."

"George, you're so sweet to say that. We love you as much as you love us."

George reached over to Maria and hugged her close. He looked straight into her eyes and planted a kiss full on her lips. "I'd say it's time we went to bed too."

Chapter Thirty
Lightfoot Tells a Strange Story

The next morning, George headed out toward the reservation to Rob Lightfoot's home. It seemed that whatever Rob wanted to talk to him about was serious, and his guess was, he didn't want anyone to hear what he had to say to George.

Rob was sitting on his porch cleaning his rifle. He had his pipe in his mouth, and every so often, a puff of smoke came out. "Morning, George," Rob said as he took his pipe out, knocked out the contents, and put it in his front pocket.

"Good morning, and it's a beautiful one too."

"Yes, it is."

"You had something to talk to me about, Rob?"

"Yes, I do. Have a seat." He paused. "One of the girls named Valarie from our family here has told a strange story. She said a week ago, a man tried to get her to go with him to see his baby puppies. She told him she didn't want to see them. The next thing he did was offer her a Baby Ruth candy bar. She said she backed away from his truck. That's when he turned the engine off and got out of the truck and tried to force her into his truck."

"What happened next? She obviously got away."

"She said she kicked him in his private parts and ran. He began to follow her, but a car came along, and she ran up to the car to get help. He turned back and jumped into his truck and sped away."

"What did he look like? What kind of truck was he driving?"

"She said it was two-tone green. He has dark hair, bald, because his hat fell off when he tried to run after her, tall, and about my age. That was her guess."

"Where did this happen?"

"She was down near Bay City Lake, picking huckleberries. It is usually remote, but many people go to swim there, and Valarie was certainly lucky that that car came along."

"Did Valarie say who was in the car and if they saw who he was. I'll have to question them."

"I already have talked to the boys. They were drinking beer and having a good time. They were afraid they would get in trouble if they said anything about what happened. Carolyn was thankful they took her home. Her huckleberries spilled all over the ground when she sprinted away from that man."

"Valarie hasn't stopped urging me to get him. She is very upset, and so are her parents. I could say we can take care of our own, but I think there's more to this situation. This guy has brazenly attempted to kidnap and what else he may have in mind. I know you have had your hands full with someone killing and molesting young girls already, George. I believe this is the same guy."

"Hard to say, Rob, he definitely portrays the same pattern that has happened to the others. Jenny, couldn't tell, she was dead, then Anna Belle was defiled, but ended in a coma for over seven months, and now has amnesia. We never discovered who the bones that the dog found belonged to. Hanna was killed and buried out at the quarry. Marjory was killed and burned, with no evidence showing if she was molested, assaulted, or just killed. Nothing shows us what he did to get them comfortable enough to go with him. I thought it was Frank Moreno, did you know him?"

"He was the one Maria interviewed and wrote about after his stroke, right?"

"Yes, and now he's dead. But I believed it was him because Marjory's bones and necklace were found in the ashes out in the forest where Frank had his hired man cutting and clearing for a home site."

"Sick. It makes me deeply disturbed over the way Marjory or any of them were brutally killed. Burning Marjory is a sign he is getting sloppy," Rob said.

"If it wasn't Frank, then who do you think it was? There is a man who I need to talk to. Jeffery Beacom has said he would talk to him and one other suspect in his own way. He slowly gets them to spread the bull and share their secrets, over a beer or two. I'll talk to Jeffery first to see if and what he has found out."

"What about finding someone who drives an old two-tone green truck?"

"That too, in fact I do know someone who does drive one. I can't believe it could be him though because everyone likes him. He goes to church every Sunday. He's just a real nice guy. But it wouldn't hurt to check him out too."

Chapter Thirty-One
Frank's Girls Return

It had been over a month since the girls, Alicia and Rose, daughters of the deceased Frank Moreno, had returned to the city of Detroit. They were pleased to have something to remember their real father, something to hold in their hearts. In spite of their mother's attitude toward Frank, it didn't matter to them. They loved her for all that she had done for them, but their father had always sent money regularly to help support them. They held a good feeling in their hearts for their father, and now at last had something to help close the void that was there for most of their lives.

They also knew they would have to return before late September to close the home up and winterize it for the long winter months. Alicia marked the weekend they would return, September 23 on a Friday, right after school. They planned to rent a car, leave their mother home, and for once enjoy a vacation in the location known as God's Country, not a godforsaken place.

September came fast, and finally they were headed north. There had been a couple of frosts, and the leaves were turning color—oranges, golden yellows, reds, and greens. The ride near West Branch was full of glorious color in the maples and onward north. By the time, they reached the Mackinaw Bridge, their anxious anticipation of the weekend increased.

They paid the bridge toll and smiled even bigger once they were in the Upper Peninsula of Michigan.

"We're here. Let's stop at the A&P Grocery store to pick up a few things. We will need to eat and clean the home up," Rose said. So Alicia pulled the car right toward the main drag of town, where they could see several tourists still enjoying the sunshine and colors along the waterfront. Some were waiting to catch the ferry to Mackinaw Island, others were checking out the fudge.

"There it is right up on your right, Alicia. Do you see it?"

"Yes, I see the A&P store, right on the water side of the street," Alicia answered her sister. She parked the rental car and the two went in. "I want hot dogs and marshmallows and barbecue charcoal to cook out," Rose stated.

"Why not have a campfire and cook them on a stick, like we're camping out?"

"Sure, that's a good idea. And don't forget to get some soap and whatever else we will need to clean up the place."

"I think we should check to see if Dad had any soap there first, then we can get it at the Red Owl in town."

"Okay, hot dog buns, hot dogs, chips, Coco-Cola, marshmallows, mustard…"

"Hershey candy bars and Graham crackers to make s'mores," Rose piped in.

Alicia laughed and grabbed the last two items and soon they were headed north and east to Cedarville.

George ran into them later at the Red Owl and reminded them of his concern for their safety.

"You see, the real killer is still on the loose. He has killed before and will again. He is a very sick man. He also is a person who appears to be kind and good but shows his true colors when he wants to have his way. He wants to be in control. Don't trust anyone, especially one who comes on offering you anything out of the ordinary. Stay together, so he doesn't catch you alone."

"Thanks, Sheriff George, we will take your advice seriously and stick to the house, swim, clean, and have a campfire tonight."

"Make sure you have a flashlight with you in case it gets dark before you are done outdoors. Do you have a flashlight?"

They looked at each other and both said no at the same time.

"Here, let me lend you one. You can return it when you are done. Going to church Sunday morning? You can return it then."

"Okay, we usually go to the Union Church, is that where you go?"

"No, I have always gone to the Lutheran Church on the hill."

"We'll meet you there."

Alicia and Rose were so tired from the trip up that they unpacked and fell into bed early. The next morning, Rose was awake before Alicia, understanding that the driver would need more sleep. Rose ate a quick piece of toast and began cleaning quietly so her sister could rest. Wiping down cupboards, dusting, and running the hand sweeper back and forth over the big braided rug in the area where the fireplace and a couple of chairs and couch sat. It was a lovely room with a huge fireplace that was made of stone. It reached all the way through the upstairs on the west wall surrounded with a horse-shoe-shaped landing, where Alicia slept.

Alicia came out of the bedroom and stretched, yawned, and said, "Do I smell toast burning?"

"An hour ago, I've been doing chores until you woke. How do you feel now?"

"Rested. I think George is all wet. I slept well and no one upset it with breathing in my face."

"Alicia, he was trying to be kind and wanted to warn us that anything is possible. I thought once I did smell cigarette smoke in the night. I sat up and looked out the window. The moon was shining bright enough to show the entire lawn down to the lake."

"So?"

"I didn't see anyone. It could have been my imagination."

"What's for breakfast, coffee?"

"There's some instant. I'll heat some water. Come on down."

The girls spent the entire day cleaning. Finally, they were pooped. "Let's rest, build a fire, and have our cookout and camp out experience. We can rest a while, until it gets dark then get ready for morning. We'll drain the pipes and lock up everything, including the work shed where Dad stored his outdoor tools, and the chairs we will sit on in the morning."

"Great! I'm all for that, Alicia."

Although Alicia was the oldest, Rose had a certain sense of responsibility and insight. She didn't tell her sister she saw cigarette butts on the lawn, in a spot where there was a vantage point to look up at the home and see what was going on. She also noticed sand tracks up to the door from that spot. She was sure someone had tried the door to see if it was locked after they had gone to bed. Fortunate for them, it was.

Was this her imagination? The butt had Camel brand written on it—a cigarette that had been only half smoked and tossed down on the grass. She chalked it up to luck that they hadn't been disturbed in their sleep and shrugged it off. Tomorrow morning they would leave for the winter and not return until spring.

The smell of the campfire and hot dogs roasting slowly, clamped in a square wire holder with a very long handle hung over the fire at the right distance to keep them from burning. While Alicia had this chore, Rose brought out the mustard, buns, and the ingredients for s'mores and sat them on a side table between the chairs.

The two sat silently after the delicious dinner and watched the fire smoldering into hot coals, long after dark. The cool dampness of fall settled in.

They quickly stirred the coals to make sure the fire would go out and maneuvered their way back into the house with the help of George's flashlight.

They were exhausted. Rose not only locked and barred the huge front door, but she went to each window and checked them to make sure they were locked.

The next morning, they waited in the churchyard to see George to return the flashlight. The car was packed and the plan was to leave right after the service. They had closed the shutters and locked them from the ground floor outdoors. The pipes were drained. She packed what was left of the food to give it to George for his family.

"Here he comes now, with Maria, Susie, and young George. He's so cute."

"George or young George is cute?"

"Young George, goof." They both laughed.

Alicia gave George the flashlight and the small bag of food explaining what it was.

"Thank you. Headed out now or?"

"Oh, no, we'll stay and leave after the service."

Rose followed George back to his car while he put the bag in it. "Sheriff, I need to tell you about something." She told him about the cigarettes, the tracks, and her being awakened when she smelled the cigarette smoke.

* * * * *

Matt was packing his personal things. He would live in Frank's cabin now that he had sold his home. It hadn't taken long. The ad was put in the Detroit newspaper to avoid anyone knowing his business in the local area. He had someone answer it through the address he had in the advertisement. They said they would be up in the area on the following weekend. The letter also stated they would pay the price of four thousand dollars if he included the furniture. They included a phone number to call if he agreed. He had forty acres that went with the home, so he was happy to get it and let everything go except his personal items.

The following weekend, Mr. and Mrs. Ferrero had arrived midmorning on Saturday. They stated they stayed in St. Ignace in a motel on the bay where they could see Mackinaw Island when they looked out the east window.

"There's something I want you to consider. Will you mind if I leave my old truck for you to rattle around here on the back roads? My intentions are to buy a new truck with some of the money you give me."

"Not at all," Vincent Ferrero said. "It's a bargain." He smiled and shook his hand.

He remembered how he had promised to lock the door and hang the keys to the cabin and the truck on a nail in the shed inside next to the door. So now he was packing. His friend Andre Tolouse had helped him get a ride to Sault Ste. Marie to purchase a new truck.

Andre was a bit of a kook, a pint short, but he was okay for something like this. When he asked Andre to help him, he said, "What's in it for me?"

The sale of the cabin left ample money for an emergency. He almost loved Frank and his daughters for giving him the cabin and skidder.

Matt had skipped church that morning. He had so many things to do. He needed to pack and move into the cabin.

He stuffed his clothes in paper bags from the grocery store. He always had extras because he always folded them neatly and slid them between the cupboard and the stove. One at a time, he packed his shirts. He carried the bag out to his new truck with his jeans in another. His overalls and jackets were placed in the cab, along with shoes on the floorboard. Now he had the dresser full of t-shirts, underwear, socks, and handkerchiefs. And his treasures he had saved in a cigar box. He always said he would buy a nice wooden box with a latch and lock on it. Well, now he could afford to buy one.

He took out the cigar box. Leaned back on the bed and opened it. The strand of long black curly hair, which he had bound with a pink rubber band, the large toe with red fingernail polish on the nail, the toe had dried out but the polish was intact. Just the memory of each item brought back that old feeling he enjoyed while in the act of satisfaction and control. His eyes held a look of desire. A desire so strong he needed to do it all over again. His toys signified every experience he had enjoyed to the fullest. He put everything back in his box and wrapped a huge rubber band around it twice. This would safely keep it together until he took time to replace the cigar box.

As he backed out of the fenced yard, he took inventory one more time—all items were in the truck. He locked the side door of the house, locked up the old truck, hung the keys inside the shed, and turned the wooden shutter on the door so it would stay shut when it was windy or stormy. He sighed. He had had at least two good memories in this old place that his father bought, and he had inherited. *Good old Dad, I miss him, and Mom too.*

Chapter Thirty-Two
Revelation at the Snows

George drove out to the Snows Channel early Sunday morning before the family was awake. He needed time to think. He stood at the waters' edge and looked out where he last saw his buddy Two Shoes. The peaceful scene of the water and Marquette Island in the distance delivered calm to George.

His mind went to all the suspects he had talked to. Chet Wilson was a prime interest up until George had taken him on that ride. He had watched for reactions at each place he had stopped to look at. He came to the conclusion that Chet was not the evil one.

On the other hand Maxwell Stewart, a man with two first names, had given him a run for his money. Yes, he liked younger women but not little girls. He was wealthy, handsome, with a good personality and a lot of good sense. Why would he stoop so low as to hunt down and step in for lust, power, and the kill?

Garde Kengas, his third suspect, talked straight, opened his home to George, and shared his hobby with him. He seemed honest to the core. George was in awe at the many things he created. *Garde just didn't seem like a killer. But who knows it has been said you can't tell a book by its cover.*

The visit to Andre's cabin was enlightening with all the pelts hanging and the crude way he lived. He was a simple man who was easily pleased. Being this simple, he didn't have the mind to be cunning or devious. Andre lived a quiet simple life without thinking about other things.

George looked across the water where Two Shoes was discovered so many years earlier. George asked himself what was he doing here, standing and looking across the Snows Channel. Why was he here?

The words came to him slowly and clearly as though someone was standing right beside him, "Remember, George, it's always the last person you would truly suspect. Remember?"

He turned on his heel and walked up the slightly sloping grade to his car with an enthusiastic smile on his face for now he knew who he had to search out and catch.

While he was in church, George half listened to the sermon. He had thoughts of what his next move would be to discover the evil one. His mind wandered to the fact that he planned to question the one man he hadn't suspected. He needed to set up a time that was convenient for him but not too far in the future. Someone had watched the Moreno girls. His hunch was it could have been that person. What stopped him from totally believing it was him was the fact that he had such a good personality and showed compassion for his boss when he had his stroke, and other times when he had helped out in an emergency. Like the time there was fire out on the Swede Road. He helped in every way he could by carrying buckets in the bucket line and throwing water on the barn to try to save it. Then there was his kindness to the children at church. He always had a mint wrapped in his pocket, offering one to the child who took time to talk to him as they left from church or in the parking lot.

He shook his head when the sound of the organ brought him back from his wandering thoughts. He noticed the Moreno girls leave. Nodding, he waved across the church at them. He took young George's hand and walked out with the family, shook the minister's hand, and told him it was a good service.

Pastor smiled back at him with a knowing look.

Dinner was over later that afternoon. Maria sat embroidering a pillowcase. Susie read a Nancy Drew mystery. She was going to be a lawmaker like her father, Susie had told him once. Young George was playing with his tractor. George could hear him humming like a motor as he drove it all over his bedroom floor.

He thought of going into the office and go over his notes. This would be a quiet time to himself to think clearly about each interview, each suspect he had talked to. He stood up and looked out to find it was raining. I'll do it tomorrow, he decided, and sat down, turned on the lamp, and read the Bible.

* * * * *

The next morning, he read the notes on his visit to Andre Tolouse as it happened.

The entry read, "The drive out to Andre Tolouse's home was fresh. The rain seemed to clean the air. Leaves had begun to fall. After a couple frosts, they would be gone. Depending on whether this fall would bring an Indian summer for a week or two, winter would come soon."

Andre's place was the last drive before a curve heading back to the west on Webb Road. He noticed the mailbox out next to the road was in need of repair. The mailbox post it was nailed to had been hit possibly with the snow plow and leaned to the north.

The drive was long and narrow heading east to the set of buildings that turned to the north before George stopped in front of the house between it and the barn to his left.

Andre met him on the porch. "What d'you want, George Kaughman?" His voice had a strong French accent.

"Good morning to you, Andre. I'm in the area and wished to take a few minutes to ask you something about a hunch I have. Maybe you can help me."

Impressed that George was asking for his help, he stepped back and said, "Come in, I'm just to eat my breakfast."

He held up the coffeepot that sat on the big cast-iron wood stove, and asked George, "Coffee?"

"Thanks, I guess I will."

Andre poured it and sat back down to eat his porridge with chopped apples, raisins, and walnuts on top. He reached for the pint-sized canning jar of honey and added a large spoonful and a little milk from the tiny pitcher to finish his cereal. He made the sign of the cross and said, "Amen."

He looked up at George and asked, "So what you want to talk about?"

"What religion are you, Andre?"

"That a funny question. Everybody know I'm Hebrew."

George had never seen Andre Tolouse and was surprised at his tiny frame. When he finally smiled, he noticed he had one tooth missing in front.

"I've always been curious. What do you do around here to survive? While I have never met you personally, my curiosity has had me wondering."

"I show you. You see, I hunt the deer, fox, and sometimes bear. I put out the bait. They come, and I shoot them." He scraped the last bite of cereal, put it in his mouth that was already full, and got up.

He went into the room next to the kitchen, with a slanted roof, where George could see bear, deer, and fox hides hanging. Andre came back with his hands full, put his wares on the kitchen table, and began his demonstration. "This I make with the antlers of the deer." He displayed a beautiful hunting knife, which had a carved deer in the handle. "This I make with the hide." Gripped with one hand was a pair of moccasins, which had woven buckskin laces. "I make the fur hat with the fox." He displayed a beautiful necklace made of bear claws and beads.

"Andre, this is good work, how do you sell it?"

"That's my secret. I have a man who buy everything I make. He takes it to the market and sells it. I don't care, I like to live peaceful and alone. Come here, I show you." He wiggled his finger to George to follow him into the shed.

George was amazed when he looked at the knives setting on a bench all lined up. Each knife had a different design and size. The same with the items he made with the deer and fox.

They were lined neatly along the walls. Tobacco pouches of the deer hide and bear skin. The knives and necklaces were pristine.

"I see you keep yourself busy. What do you do in your spare time?"

"Eh, man, are you deaf? I do this all the time. I keep here or hunt. Not go unless it necessary."

"You sure have impressed me with your wonderful work, Andre. One more question, Andre. I was told you were in Sault Ste. Marie recently, is this true?"

"Yes, I went with a friend to buy who bought a new truck."

"Was it Matthew Dillon?"

"Yes, it was, we just bought the truck and drove home. I drove the old one and he drove his new one."

"I guess you have answered my question."

"What about your hunch?"

"I was wondering if you ever go out to the quarry. Someone said you were seen there.

"Like always, here."

"Okay, Andre. Thank you and keep up the good work. Can you tell me who the man is that you sell your wears to?"

"Like I say, it's my secret. That's what I say, better to not talk to anyone. When you're nice that's when *poof*, they accuse you."

"No one's accusing you, Andre, I'm just speculating. That's my job."

"I like mine better. Your job is dangerous."

George took his hat from the kitchen table and left. But not before he saw a two-tone green truck parked in the barn. George had written it as he remembered it that evening. He still could see no reason to suspect him.

* * * * *

Since it was Monday, there was little chance he would find Matt home, but he decided to drive that way anyway. He saw the boarded fence surrounding the house before he saw that the two-tone green truck was sitting in Matt's yard.

Two trucks the same in the exact vicinity of the Les Cheneaux area? Now that's a coincidence. Matt must be sick or has not found work with the mill yet. He did miss church yesterday.

George got out of his car and approached the house. No one answered when he knocked. He peered through the window to see what he could. The place looked different. What was it? Clean? No, empty. The furniture was there, but the usual items that sat on the cupboards and the table were gone. But the truck is sitting here. Where was Matt?

He walked out to the back yard. He noticed his garden was completely harvested and all the vines and weeds were pulled out and piled. He walked out and around the shed. There would be tracks since the fresh rain the day before.

Adrenaline rushed in George's system. He immediately believed Matt or whatever his name was had taken a powder. But you can't vanish into thin air; he wasn't Houdini.

Then he remembered that Andre said Matt bought a new truck.

George drove back to Andre's acreage. He noticed he was still there. He heard a shot come from the direction of the woods. Then George heard laughter and Andre talking to someone. "I got you and you thought you'd get away from me, didn't you?" Then cracking of branches, and Andre emerged from the woods dragging a big black bear.

Andre noticed George quickly and asked, "You back here?"

"Yes, I forgot one thing I needed to ask you."

"What was that?"

"Are you aware that you aren't the only one with a two-tone green Ford truck pickup around here?"

"Sure, I know."

"What do you know?"

"I know someone else has a two-tone Ford in this area."

"Who is it?" George had to know if Andre knew Matt.

"My friend who bought the new truck the other day has a two-toned green pickup. His name is Matt Dillon."

* * * * *

George heard his radio squawk in and out. George couldn't tell what it said, but more often than not, it was important. He said, "Excuse me, I need to get back to civilization to get this message. I'll be back as quickly as I can to finish this conversation."

"I be here when you come back."

George drove to a high clearing and tried to get the sheriff's office in St. Ignace.

The message came back. "Yes, George, you need to get with Rob Lightfoot, he has an urgent message for you."

"Got it, I'll get right on it."

He drove in the direction of the reservation. There he saw Rob Lightfoot coming out of the community center.

"What's happened, Rob?"

"Valarie is missing. She promised she wouldn't go with that man in the two-toned green pickup. If she has gone with him, she was abducted. I need you to help me find her. She came up missing Saturday night."

"What did her parents tell you?"

"They said Valarie said she was going for a walk. She promised to be back before dark. George, you must understand Valarie, she loves nature, and she seems to cling to the old ways, even though times have changed from the times when we were young. On her walks, she would watch birds and enjoy seeing wild game, not for food but the many ways they lived and migrated. She studied the seasons and weather by the animals actions and life. A walk to her was part of her education. So Saturday, when she didn't show up before dark, her parents knew there was foul play. Everyone on the tribe that was available traced her footprints and couldn't find her. However, they did find her footprints and another one bigger, showing the two as though they were struggling. We're sure she is with him, the evil one."

"It sounds as though he was waiting for her, watching and waiting. I have a hunch, but I have to be absolutely sure. This guy is a sociopath, who convinces everyone he is a wonderful man, yet he has a dark side. If I'm right, I'll have him as quickly as I can. I would ask you to come with me, but I have to do this on my own. He would figure out right away what was coming down if he saw you. He's actually a bully. He can handle a child but can't face a man. He uses women and small children for his own purpose. I'm hot on the trail, and I hope I can find him before he does anything to Valarie. With the help from our Creator, we will solve the crime and abduct the perpetrator."

"Okay, George, I'll go along with your plan and sit on my hands until I hear from you. Pray to Gizhe-Manadoo, our creator."

He nodded and left. George stopped in to his office to get his notes. He had the camera and a few items he had in the evidence box. He wanted to quickly go over the few items he had to go on, one in particular that would convince him that he was the one. He wasn't sure, but he was close. First, he would go back to Andre's. He was so close to getting something from him, and he knew it was important.

Maria saw him poking around in his office and came across. "George, I took a call from Ralph Carter. When Ralph called, he needed to talk to you as soon as you possibly could get over there."

"Can't it wait, honey? I'm really on something big right now."

"It's up to you, but if it was me, I'd go. It really sounded urgent."

"It's in the direction I'm going anyway, so I'll stop over. Tell them that if they call back."

She reached up and kissed him and gave him a quick hug, then watched his back as he left.

The drive to Carter's farm went quickly; soon he was driving up the sand drive.

Martha answered the door. "Come in, please take a seat here. I'll call Ralph." She stepped out on the porch and pulled the cord of the dinner bell.

Ralph hurried as soon as he heard it. He popped through the door smiling when he saw George's car in the yard. "Hi, George, good you could come this fast."

"What has happened that you found it an emergency, Frank?"

"It's Anna Belle. It started about a month ago with terrible nightmares. She would wake up screaming. We would go in to see what she was screaming about, and she would be crying but couldn't remember. This has been happening more frequently, and she is remembering bits and pieces of what happened to her."

"Do you mind if I talk to her?"

"She is here because I kept her home today. She put in such a horrific night, I felt she needed the rest."

"Anna Belle, come down to talk to George. He is here to help you if he can with your dreams."

"I'm not a doctor, and you do have to go and let him know what has happened. But I will listen and try to make something out of what is happening."

Anna Belle heard his last sentence and sat next to him. She was scared to death. "Sheriff George, I am starting to remember what happened to me over a year ago. I remember I got off the school bus and began walking in the direction of our farm. This truck came along and drove slowly beside me. He asked me if I had a dog and did I like dogs."

"I told him yes, I did have a dog and three cats, and I loved all four of them. Then he asked me if I wanted to see his new puppies. He convinced me it was close, so it wouldn't take long and he would bring me home afterward. I got in the truck." She hesitated.

"What color or make was the truck?" George asked her.

"I'm not sure the make, but it was light green on top and dark green on the bottom."

"Think closely, Anna Belle, did it have the letters *F-O-R-D* on it?"

"I can't remember."

"So you got in the truck, what happened next?"

"We drove here and there, and the short trip had me confused, I wasn't sure where I was. When he drove in his place, the first thing I remember was his house was small, not like Daddy's and Mommy's farmhouse. Then he said the puppies are around back of the woodshed. When I got there, I realized he didn't have a dog. He grabbed me and tried to kiss me. I struggled, and he called me baby doll, and said, 'That's it, baby doll, fight me, I want you to.' He dragged me into the house and threw me on the bed. I passed out in fear. When I woke, he was gone. I bolted out the door and didn't realize I only had one shoe on. My clothes were torn, and I hurt all over. I ran and ran down to the end of the road and across the field into the woods. It was getting dark, I ran so much I was getting exhausted. I was light-headed and weak, yet the fear kept me going. Finally, the moon came through the clouds just long enough to spot a hollow log. I pulled the moss away and crawled as far up into it as I could, then I covered myself with the moss. Everything went black. The next thing I remember was Mom in the room, a strange room but a sunny room."

"What kind of shoe were you wearing Anna Belle?"

"It was a saddle shoe, brown and white."

"Thank you, Anna Belle." He looked up to the Carters and said, "Take her into the doctor right away. She needs to talk to him and get help."

"I know he hurt me terribly, I just know it, but I can't remember."

Martha reached to her and hugged her. "All in good time, honey, when you're ready. God will help you through this."

George stood and said he had to go for now but would check back in a couple of days. He patted Anna Belle on the shoulder and said, "You did a good job remembering. Don't be afraid anymore. Everything will be all right."

He walked quickly to his car and drove fast as he could to Andre's. He found him in the room where he does his work.

George could see Andre had skinned the bear, where it hung drying out. He could smell the formaldehyde he had used to cure it.

"Andre, I came back since I left in the middle of our conversation."

"Three times, and I won't have company again until my buyer comes again."

"Yes, well, you were saying Matt Dillon has a truck like yours?"

"I didn't say it was his."

"I was sure you did. Where did he get the money to buy a new truck?"

"He said he sold his forty acres with the house."

Now the pieces of the puzzle began to fit. "Tell me everything, Andre, I need to hear it."

"Since you're the sheriff around here, I suppose I should. I'll never get any rest until I do. He came over and asked me to take him to the Sault because he wanted to buy a new truck."

George waited patiently, but his insides were rushing himself as well as his patience was going fast. He had to save Valarie, before it was too late.

"What else can you tell me? Did he move out yet? Where was he going? What kind of truck did he buy? Did he say if he was moving away and if so how far?"

"Hey, buddy, you giving me too many questions at one time."

He thought a minute then began his narration. "We left about nine in the morning, went to the Chevrolet dealers. He really liked the new one that just came out, a good one for off the roads. He is a timber man and is off roads most of the time. We went for a test drive and ate lunch while we were testing it out at Clyde's Car Hop.

That was the best hamburger ever, except the one's at the Runway Bar right close to home. Then we went back, around, say, eleven, and he said he wanted it just the way it was. The dealer started to write out the papers and seemed impatient and said, 'I don't need papers, just how much? I have the money here.' He pulled out a wad that was the most money I ever saw in one setting. *Sacré bleu!* But the dealer said he had to write the contract out anyway. So we waited. It was his lunchtime, and he excused himself and sent in another dealer to finish them out.

"By now it's one o'clock. So I tell him, 'I'm going to head back. He knew the way without me.' He gave me a dark look and shrugged his shoulders and threw up his hands in the air. I haven't seen him since."

"So what color did he settle on?"

"It is white so the sand won't show, he said. But it will, and no one will see him coming this winter when the ground is covered with snow."

In spite of everything, George had to smile. "Thanks, Andre, for relating to me the whole day getting the truck. You have a good day."

Chapter Thirty-Three
The Evil One

George drove away thinking he needed to get over to the home where Matt lived, check out any indication that Valarie may have been hurt worse, some blood or hair, traces of struggle at his home. Perhaps that was why it looked so clean. He used the key that hung in the shed to open the door and walked through the small home quickly, not regarding anything unusual. He went out to the shed and checked the contents, when he noticed the truck key on the nail next to the door. He grabbed the truck keys and rushed to unlock it. Once he was in the truck, he slowed down and took each inch of the interior slowly. A part of her shirt was ripped off and the patch sat on the seat. He did struggle with her. He examined the seat closer for a sign of blood, but to his relief, he didn't find much else. There was a wide roll of tape, which made George imagine she was taped across her mouth and wrists. Only time would tell, and time was on Matt's side right now. George felt he had wasted enough time trying to catch him and prove beyond a reasonable doubt is was him, and only him, who did all these horrible things. He knew he had to check the cabin that the Moreno girls gave Matt.

He pulled away from Matt's old home and headed toward the woods and the little cabin. Heading north and west through the pines and cedars, the trees changed to maples, birch, oak, and poplar, a rare beech, here or there showed up. He crossed a cedar patch and a small creek with a bridge built with cedar posts and rock sand. Soon he could see the tiny log cabin. There was smoke traveling out the chimney as the day had turned cold and dark. He stopped down the path, hidden by the wooded area, and he walked up to the cabin. No one was around. No sign of a new truck either. George crept up to the cabin and looked inside the dirty window. He peered closely and saw what appeared to be a person sitting on a straight chair. It was Valarie. He put his finger to his lips when she saw him to tell her to be quiet, yet her eyes showed fear. He peered through another window to make absolutely sure she was alone in the cabin. He came through the door with his gun drawn and ready to shoot if Matt was there.

Looking around the one room facility, he rested assured that the girl was alone. But he knew he had to save her quickly and get away. Gently removing the tape from her mouth, he said, "Don't say anything until we are safely out of here."

Tears came to her eyes and she nodded. Matt had taken her long braids and cut them off right up to her head. He laid them on the table. As George and Valarie left the cabin, she grabbed her braids and ran to the sheriff car. Since George had not seen Matt on his way in, he took the same trail out.

Once they were down the trail and on the road back to the reservation, George asked her to tell him everything.

"Start where you told your mom and dad that you were taking a walk and would be back before dark."

"Okay, I was walking along, enjoying hearing the mockingbirds, and the brook alongside the road. I stopped to see if there were any minnows swimming in the one spot where the creek had washed out, and it was a little deeper. It was over a mile away from home. I could hear the engine and crunching of gravel as the truck came near me. I began walking, and it stayed steady with my pace. He cranked the window down. 'Hey, aren't you the papoose I talked to the other day, and you kicked me in the groin?' he asked me. I answered, 'I don't remember.' He seemed angry, stopped, and jumped out he grabbed and forced me into the truck. My blouse ripped, and he jerked the piece off that hung there. I began to scream, and he grabbed tape and put it over my mouth, then he taped my hands so I couldn't get away.

"I knew he had bad things in mind, but I never thought it would be this bad. He drove to his house and parked. Next thing, he pulled me out and jerked me toward his new truck. I was sure he was going to kill me when he pulled and jerked me toward the other truck. It was white and new. He pushed me into the front passenger seat and bound my feet together and left me there while he locked the old truck and hung the key in the old shed. It was then I realized he had changed trucks.

"After he locked the truck and hung the key in the shed someplace we drove away. I sat knowing I couldn't get away. Even if I ran, he would catch me. There was no one around that place. It was desolate. Soon we came to the cut off to the log cabin. Once there, he dragged me into the cabin and taped me to the chair. He grabbed a sharp knife, and I thought he was going to stab me to death. He looked at me and said, 'This is for kicking me in the groin.' That's when he grabbed my braid roughly and cut it off, then the other one. He threw them on the table. I thanked my Creator that I was still alive. Next he cut away the tape from the chair and my wrists. He threw me on the bed. He roughly pulled my jeans off while I screamed and struggled he had his way. After it was over, he put my jeans back on and taped me to the chair again. He mumbled, 'If you're good, I won't kill you.' Then he left and you came. I am so grateful you did."

"How old are you, Valarie?"

"I just had my twelfth birthday. I'm a little big for my age, but now I'm ruined. I am so ashamed. I broke my promise to my parents."

"Hey, little one, hush, it will be all right. We'll catch him, and he will be punished for what he has done to you and all the ones he has defiled."

"When you called me 'little one,' I remember, he called me baby doll."

* * * * *

Rob Lightfoot walked out of his log cabin home to see George driving up with Valarie. He jumped off his porch half laughing; he was so relieved to see her. Her hair, he thought, but what else? She is a strong young girl, and she is also a survivor.

"Let's call your parents. It's time to celebrate."

"Not until I catch that monster," George replied. "Take her to her parents. I must keep on it in case he tries to escape."

"Thank you, George, I'm very grateful," Lightfoot said. Valarie hugged him. "I am too."

George radioed the Mackinaw Sheriff's Office to send an all-points bulletin out for Matt Dillon, who probably had an alias, driving a new white Ford pickup.

* * * * *

Meanwhile, Matt had a few things to do at the camp where he was working. It was near dark when he headed back to the log cabin. He put his tools away and placed the keys to the skidder safely in his pocket. He looked around and thanked the Chard Mill for giving him work.

He also thanked his lucky stars for the little charm he had back at the cabin. The desire that he looked forward to encouraged him to speed up and get back to her.

He drove up to the cabin, stepped out, and entered the door. Immediately he saw that Valarie was gone. He screamed and threw the chair across the tiny room. He took off his hat and pulled on what hair he had left and shouted curses aloud, while they echoed across the clearing. That was when he heard the revolver click in place. His heart jumped, and he transferred his personification into the charmer. "Who can I say is calling on me out here in the woods?"

"It's I, Sheriff George," George said with a steady determined voice. "I'm taking you in on multiple charges of murder."

"Do you have proof?"

"All I need. You see, Anna Belle saw you every Sunday until she finally remembered what you did to her, and today I rescued Valarie, who agreed you were the same person who violated her as well."

George knew it wouldn't be hard to cuff this meek person who kept saying, "I'm the wrong one. I never did those terrible things. I'm innocent."

George held up the cigar box of Matt's treasures and said, "With this box of evidence, you will go to jail for a lifetime for all the murders you have committed. Not only the crimes you committed in my jurisdiction, but God knows where else during your life." Matt hung his head and became silent.

George thanked his Heavenly Father, Gizhe-Manidoo, for helping him save at least two of the six girls. He gave his creator all the glory when he captured the evil one. Rob had called him *maji-mani-doo*, one who does an evil act. The very one who had abducted and murdered several young girls.

By the time George took Matt into the county sheriff's jail, wrote the report, and drove back home, it was well past midnight. He was greeted by his beautiful wife, who hugged him and fed him. "We'll talk in the morning," he said as he sat on the bed and took off his shoes and socks.

* * * * *

A celebration was planned by Rob Lightfoot. He rejoiced in the saving of young Valarie. George supplied a list of all those who had come in contact or were a part of those who were victimized or murdered. This included those who were instrumental in catching the killer, the evil one.

By now his name was in the past. It was time to forget and forgive. It was time to move on with life and enjoy being together with those who chose to. They were prepared to find happiness as it was presented to them in each individual case.

The community center was the designated gathering place. George and Lightfoot built a fire pit for a whole hog roast and provided it to prepare for the celebration. It was decided a potluck would work for the remaining meal. Maria arrived with Susie and George Jr., next Jane and Gordon Adams and their children arrived, and soon one family at a time arrived until the center was as full as it had ever been. Many took seats and gathered around the fire pit. Frank the timber contractor's daughters arrived surprising the entire crowd. Valarie wore a navy kerchief over her hair, as it hadn't gown out yet. Never-the-less she was beautiful. She clung to Lightfoot as though he was her hero.

Vincenza had allowed the 'Americans' to call her 'Ginny' so as she and Bill Catolica drove into the parking lot, someone shouted, "Here comes Ginny with a whole pile of pies."

Rob Lightfoot banged a metal spoon against a pot to get attention from everyone. As everyone had quieted down, he began, "Good afternoon. It is indeed a good afternoon for this gathering. I wish to give a big thanks to George Kaughman for doing his duty and catching the man who has had our community stirred up in fear for more than a few years. Now we can get back to feeling free to return to our daily lives and know Sheriff George is here for us." Lightfoot pointed to George.

Everyone whistled and clapped for George.

The children could smell the delicious odor of the pork roast and felt their stomach growl. So could others but waited patiently for a response from George.

"Thank you for your greeting, and thank you, Rob, as well. All I did was my job. I'm happy to be here and happy you are here also. Let's enjoy our time here today and make it a good day to remember. Shall we bow our heads in thanks to our Heavenly Father and Creator for all his gifts we are about to receive."

The room became silent as all bowed their heads in gratitude.

"Thank you, dear Creator, for all our blessings, for those who are here and those who couldn't be. Thank you for this food that you have provided. Amen."

The food, conversation, games, laughter, and happiness made this day one to remember.

Epilogue

During the course of research before the trial of Matt Dillon, alias Clarence Grimshaw, it was discovered that he had murdered several young teenagers from the area he had lived formerly. Old cases had been reopened and evidence studied indicating that he had used the same familiar pattern of his foul actions leading up to the young ladies' demise. One of them had a missing toe, which matched the one of his treasures in the old cigar box. More research led to the solution to these cases as well. It was found that his parents protected him and lied for him while they were alive. This enabled him to do more heinous crimes. Finally, many of the criminal justice personnel believed or questioned if he had in fact killed his own parents.

Anna Belle's schoolbag was found in the old shed where the evil one hid it along with many other items too big to fit in a cigar box. Anna Belle continued her high school years, graduated, and was married to the neighbor who was just a few years older than her. He attended the Celebration Barbeque.

Frank Moreno's daughters moved to the Les Cheneaux area the next summer and entered the College in the Soo. They graduated and remained in the home near the water. At twenty-five, they donated part of their inheritance to enlarge the school in Cedarville. After college, they became teachers at the school and stayed in the area.

George Kaughman remained sheriff and hired Jeffery Beacom as an assistant. He was recognized as a hero in the investigation of the serial killer.

Valarie continued to study nature and became a wildlife agent in the tricounty area. Her mother took her journey to be with our Creator. Valarie remained near her father and took care of him. Rob Lightfoot lived next door to the family and kept close, watch over them and the entire reservation with great care.

About the Author

Audrey J. Fick (A. Jay) is a longtime resident of the Eastern Upper Peninsula of Michigan, as well as a graduate of Lake Superior State University. Her Bachelor of Science leaned toward a creative writing and crime writing degree. She has been a feature writer for *The St. Ignace News* since 2007. She was a fiction editor for the fifth edition of *Border Crossing*, an international literary journal. Her book review of Mark Jacob's *Forty Wolves* was published in the September 2015 edition of *Peace Corp Magazine*. She currently lives in Hessel, Michigan.